'Nobody knew wh... been there, ten-foot pyramids of stones as big as your head. Some said the old stone-wallers had built them. Some said they were older than the stone-wallers . . .'

As Ralph leans over to put back some fallen stones from one of the ancient cairns on the top of Fiend's Fell, he notices a strange piece of yellowish metal sticking out. It's too yellow for aluminium but too pale for brass. Intrigued, he begins to dig until he discovers something a bit like a car windscreen. But this is no car – it's some sort of glass or perspex dome. And inside the dome Ralph can see what looks like a body . . .

This is only the beginning of Ralph's chilling adventure, as strange supernatural forces invade the quiet, unsuspecting farming community in which he lives.

Robert Westall was born in 1929 in Tynemouth. He spent two years with the Royal Signals between studying for degrees at Durham and London Universities. He then taught in a sixth form college in Cheshire before opening an antique shop. He has since given up the shop to become a full time writer. Robert Westall is one of today's best known writers for young people and has twice won the Carnegie Medal.

Other books by Robert Westall

URN BURIAL

Robert Westall

Penguin Books

PENGUIN BOOKS

Published by the Penguin Group
Penguin Books Ltd, 27 Wrights Lane, London W8 5TZ, England
Penguin Books USA Inc., 375 Hudson Street, New York, New York 10014, USA
Penguin Books Australia Ltd, Ringwood, Victoria, Australia
Penguin Books Canada Ltd, 10 Alcorn Avenue, Toronto, Ontario, Canada M4V 3B2
Penguin Books (NZ) Ltd, 182–190 Wairau Road, Auckland 10, New Zealand

Penguin Books Ltd, Registered Offices: Harmondsworth, Middlesex, England

First published by Viking Kestrel 1987
Published in Penguin Books 1989
10 9 8 7 6 5 4

Copyright © Robert Westall, 1987
All rights reserved

Printed in England by Clays Ltd, St Ives plc
Filmset in Photina

For all the higher mammals that trusted man
And got betrayed.

CHAPTER 1

Ralph finished storing his gear in the top-box of the scrambler-bike. A jar of Stockholm tar, a bottle of cold tea, butties wrapped up tight in his anorak to keep the tar smell out of them.

The sheepdogs were waiting, keeping their eye in, herding the free-range hens round the farmyard and up the outside stair of the barn, from which they flew down squawking in a cloud of feathers; which sent the collies into their loll-tongued grins.

The scrambler started third kick; first crisis of the day over. Ralph distrusted, hated, all machinery. But he had to use the scrambler. The trip up Fiend's Fell took too long on foot. He turned out of the farmyard, skidded on the pool of cow-dung at the corner, and shot up on to the green-road.

The green-road zigzagged up the fell between black stone walls, lined with last year's bracken, high and brown. This year's bracken, so green and new you wanted to eat it, was just curling through to take possession.

Ralph's heart lifted. It was good to be up and away on the fell. But the turf of the green-road was slashed and rutted by the other shepherds' scramblers, and the explosions of his own engine blatted back from the black stone walls, spoiling the peace. Everything was getting spoilt these days. He looked down on the village, tight huddle of grey houses that had stood so right for so long. But spoilt by those shiny metal barns and silos; the straggle of new red-brick bungalows leading nowhere. What did rich folk want to live in the country for?

But it was great to climb up into the quiet; with the dogs racing alongside, or taking short-cuts over the walls to keep up.

A mile on, he parked, put on his anorak, sandwiches in one pocket, tea and tar in the other. The top of Fiend's Fell was too much even for scramblers. Steep as a house roof, covered with tussocks of dead, blond grass bigger than pop-stars' haircuts; veined through with black burns deep as trenches and treacherously concealed by overhanging tussocks. It was hard enough to keep your feet walking;

7

sliding and panting. The only thing that moved fast on Fiend's Fell were the scatters of dirty sheep fleeing upwards before him. And the sheepdogs, tiny and black with a ruff of white at the throat, flying up like birds, not attacking the sheep but instinctively cutting them into flocks, moving them here and there from habit. Sheepdogs were like policemen, never off duty. He whistled them to heel; otherwise they'd run themselves too hot, then lie down in a burn to cool off and give themselves colic.

He kept to the wire fence, drawn like a pencil line up the fell. The sheep grazed more heavily there; shepherds walked there; the going was easier; it avoided the precipitous black burns.

But it was also depressing. Unlike stone walls, the fences gave the sheep no shelter in winter blizzards. The sheep drifted downwind, until the fences stopped them, caught in the open, and there they died. There was always a scatter of skulls along the fence; sodden, yellow fleeces laid out like hearthrugs with the bones delicately scattered on top where the carrion crows had left them. Often, a small scatter lay tangled in the big scatter, where a lamb had died with its mother.

It pained Ralph. The lowland sheep, the fat white-faced Cheviots, were cosseted in barns for the lambing, fed from hay bales in the bitter weather. The fell-sheep, the black-faced Herdwicks, were left all year to live or die. Visited annually, in August, to be counted and sheared, branded and dipped. That's what he was doing now, early in July, getting ready for the shearing. Counting the corpses, the survivors, the number of well-grown lambs, twins.

That and his own particular brand of mercy, the Stockholm tar. The sheep got whicked, see? Cut themselves on the barbed wire, or leaping wildly over stone walls in one of their sudden inexplicable panics. Then the blowflies laid their eggs in the open wounds, and the foul white grubs hatched out and began to eat the sheep alive.

He spotted their first victim, running well behind its group with a humping, rocking-horse gait, the raw red patch on its rump clearly visible in the sunlight. He sent off the dogs, Jet to the left, Nance to the right, cutting their wide circles across the tussocks, coming in from behind, penning the whole group into a corner where the fence met an old black wall.

'Coom by, Jet! Coom by, Nance!' But he was just making noises. The dogs, veterans, knew what he wanted better than he did himself. Soon, there was stillness. The sheep huddled together, staring at him hostile with their strange, oblong, yellow eyes. The dogs lay staring at the sheep, tongues lolling, edging forwards on their bellies inch by inch. Keeping the sheep just scared enough to be still; not scared enough to try a wild leap over the wall.

'Laydoon, Jet!' 'Laydoon, Nance!' He waded among the dense-packed woolly bodies that shifted uneasily; felt their sharp feet through the leather of his boots. Grabbed the victim, clenched her backwards between his knees, and reached out the Stockholm tar. It glugged, black and oily, into the red wound as big as a man's hand, and soon the evil maggots swam upwards, drowning as they died. The victim would live; the maggots hadn't reached a vital part, spine or bowel. She glared up at him with eyes that comprehended nothing but terror. He let her go, checked the rest, called off the dogs. The little flock went off like a rocket.

'I am the good shepherd,' he thought wryly. 'I know my sheep and am known of them.' He never heard that reading, sitting beside Mam in chapel, without smiling. Sheep must have been a lot brighter in Jesus' time. To these sheep he was just one more terrifying monster in their terror-stricken lives. Why? Cows came to him, pigs were friendly, even the lowland Cheviots. He knew so little of these sheep's lives. Fifty-one weeks in the year they were up here alone, in the snow and wind and rain. What went on, to make them so frightened? The top of Fiend's Fell was a lonely place, always had been. Take away the man-made fence, it might be a hundred years ago, a thousand. If he himself fell into the black gully of an overhung burn, broke his leg, would anybody ever find him? Or would his bones lie, picked white as the sheep's, till they rotted away in the beer-brown water?

He glanced around; he had dipped into a bowl of the land. All round stretched the brown swell of the fell. Apart from the fence, not a work of man in sight. He shuddered, despite the July sun.

Don't be daft; the dogs would bring help; the dogs would find him. He called them to him, looked into their warm, brown eyes, played with their floppy, velvet ears. At least he knew his sheepdogs and was known of them.

Get on; it's nearly lunch-time.

He ate it sitting against the cairn that marked the top of Fiend's Fell. The dogs, as usual, coaxed half his sandwiches out of him. Spam, cheese, pickle, they loved them all. Nosed the greaseproof paper carefully to make sure of the last crumb, then went off hunting something live for the rest of their dinner. Never still, sheepdogs. He could see their feathery, black tails waving out of some shallow burn. They moved towards each other from opposite ends, hoping to trap something tasty and stupid between them.

Overfull, he drowsed, surveying the sunlit fell through half-closed eyes. Why *Fiend's* Fell? Local people didn't call it that; just 'the fell'. But on the Ordnance Survey map at school he'd found it quite clearly named. When he asked, people just shrugged and said it was some daft idea of people in London, who'd nothing better to do . . .

Then he felt the change come. A gentle pressing against one side of his face that wasn't wind, but a new, faint, warm dampness. He knew, even though the sky was still blue, that it'd be raining before four. Heavy, maybe thunder. No fun, on the open fell in a thunderstorm. Last time, the only dry spot on him had been a two-inch patch under his belt. He'd dripped a pool in Mam's kitchen four feet wide. No shelter up on the fell, see? None at all.

Suddenly urgent, he got up to get on.

It was then he noticed some stones had fallen off the top of the cairn and were lying in the heather.

Nobody knew who'd made the cairns. They'd always been there, ten-foot pyramids of stones as big as your head. Some said the old stone-wallers had built them. Some said they were older than the stone-wallers. Some said that in the dim and distant, every shepherd starting out from the valley had brought a stone up with him, and the cairns were built that way. Certainly there were no other loose stones around for miles.

The one certainty was that if you were a shepherd you didn't let the cairns fall down. After a sudden freak blizzard, they were the only familiar things in a totally changed landscape. They looked after cairns, shepherds.

He picked up the first fallen stone, and leaned over to put it back.

Funny; there was a piece of metal sticking up, like the tip of a bricklayer's trowel set upright. It had corroded into white spots, the way aluminium does. Idly, he tried to pull it out, but it stuck fast. And it *wasn't* a bricklayer's trowel; too slim and pointed. Intrigued, he pulled out two more stones. But the thing still wouldn't budge. He could tell from the way it moved, grated against the stones, that there was a lot more of it, down inside. He pulled away more stones, laying them down careful and handy; wouldn't take long to rebuild the cairn . . .

After ten minutes he'd revealed two more feet of yellowish metal; a long pointed blade, with a thin tapered shaft below. Was it an ancient spear? But knights had used iron spears, which would've rusted. And he remembered from school the Romans used bronze. And it was definitely *fixed*, to something deep inside. He looked in distress at the topless cairn, at the stones now scattered in all directions. He looked at his watch; his lunch-hour had run out. And the rain *was* coming . . .

But he couldn't bear not to know now. Oh, well . . . he could work late . . . get wet.

After another half an hour, four feet of spear was showing, immovable as ever. Except . . . it definitely wasn't a spear . . . too whippy, modern. Not a metal he'd ever seen before. Too yellow for aluminium, too pale for brass. And the lower shaft, where it had been protected from the weather by the cairn, glistened strangely. He thought of the wireless-aerial of a tank . . .

The dogs, aware their usual routine had been broken, had come back from their search for lunch and were lying watching, heads cocked. He felt guilty about his boss; he felt guilty about the cairn. But he had to *know*. Maybe it was something for the Ministry of Defence, like the big radio-towers over towards Middleton-in-Teesdale way. But then, why hide it? Was it the *Russians*? He attacked the cairn with renewed vigour, appalled at his own powers of destruction.

Finally his hand, delving round another stone, touched something smooth and cool and rounded. He pulled away the stone and saw something a bit like a car windscreen. Darkness inside, and something inside the darkness. Now he was throwing away stones any old how, making the dogs back away to safety.

He cleared a foot of windscreen, and saw something metallic and complicated inside; lying on . . . a fur rug? He cleared more stones; saw more of the metallic thing, more fur rug. Under a glass dome; well, more like perspex, and shaped like a cigar. *Was* it the Russians? His belly crept . . .

He snatched away one more stone; half the side of the cairn collapsed.

Then he realized it wasn't just a fur rug in there. Under the rug . . . was the shape . . . of a leg . . . and a shoulder. Still half-hidden, a bump that must be . . a head.

Quite still, under the glass.

A coffin.

He leapt back. Staring at the wild, spreading destruction of the cairn, he knew he had done a dreadful thing. He stared around fearfully, expecting punishment. But no punishment came, and he felt terribly alone. He looked at the dogs, but they just looked back, puzzled why he didn't get back to work. He felt even more alone. Then he decided, if he put all the stones back very, very carefully, under that indifferent blue sky, no one would ever know and he would not be punished.

That was best.

But when he went back (careful not to look at the man wrapped inside the striped fur rug) he noticed that the coffin was in two halves, a top and a bottom. Hinged together. And at the side were three things a bit like the locks on a suitcase. Funny-shaped and far too thin, of the same yellowish metal; but he thought he could see how they worked.

One peep? Surely that wouldn't do any harm? He wrestled with his conscience; began to replace the stones.

Then undid the locks with a rush: one, two, three. They snapped back, making the coffin resound like a drum. He raised the lid a fraction.

There was no smell of foulness, like what lingered inside the sheep's skulls lying by the wire. A gentle smell, like the ointment Mam used to put on his knee when he grazed it. A *safe* smell. It gave him the courage to lift the lid, tip it back.

The snarling behind brought him out in a cold sweat.

But it was only the dogs, backing away, bellies pressed to the ground, ears flat to their skulls and the skin of their lips puckered up showing long teeth, brown at the roots. The hair on their backs was standing up in arched ridges, and their tails were bushed-up and looked enormous. And always they retreated further and further. That scared him badly; made him stop, and stand a long while motionless in the sunlight. But his nosiness was too strong. In the end, he shrugged . . . the dogs would get over it . . .

He turned back to the coffin, still reassured by the safe smell. Who was it, wrapped in the fur rug . . . if he pulled it away a little . . .

But as soon as he touched it, he realized it *wasn't* a man wrapped in a fur rug. It was only a striped, furry animal buried there. He laughed to himself a little; he'd seen plenty of dead animals . . .

But what animal? Six feet long, curled up on its side. A big cat. Like a tiger, only the stripes were fainter and narrower, brown. Too slim for a tiger. A cheetah? ... that kind of frailty and gentleness. No, too big for a cheetah. And the forepaws long and delicate, like human hands. And the hind-legs made up half the length of the whole body.

He got in close and peered at the dead face. The closed eyes had been huge, but the closed mouth quite small, less frightening than a dog's. He touched the shoulder. The fur was soft, dense, fine. The muscles were soft and supple, but intensely cold.

Then he saw the belt it was wearing, woven from the yellow metal. And the circular medallion hung round its neck. And he somehow knew it had walked upright like a man. And thought like a man. And it had never walked this earth ...

Well, not *born* here ...

Somehow he had done a dreadful thing. He just stood and shook and watched his dogs, tiny black spots now, turn on their heels and run away over the rim of the fell, heading for home.

The dogs knew he had done a dreadful thing.

He looked up at the blue sky. The blue sky looked back, indifferent. Were they up there somewhere, hidden behind the sun? Watching? Would they come? Punish?

He might have stood there shaking for ever, if his eye hadn't lit on the top of the spear, still standing upright from the coffin. He saw it with great clarity, against the blue sky; the marks of corrosion on it. It had been there a long, long time. The grave was old, old. As old as the cairn, which his grandfather had sat on as a boy. Whoever they'd been, they were gone, light-years across space.

He relaxed; his sin was his own. He could undo it, when he put back the cairn and no one need ever know. But before he did ... he was seized with a desire to know what the creature had looked like in life. He lay down on his side, next to the coffin. The sharp edges of the stones cut into his hip, as he raised both hands to the creature's dead face, so close to his own. His arms trembled, but he pushed up the eyelids, which were as cold and supple as the rest.

The creature stared at him; cat's eyes, pupils reduced to thin slits. There was a sense of hunching-up in the face, of shock, pain. The same look that he'd seen on the face of a mummified Egyptian cat, on the school trip to the British Museum. He wondered, if he turned the body over, whether he would find some terrible wound ... but that was unthinkable. He let the eyelids drop shut; smoothed their fur, where his fingers had ruffled it. Marvelled at the tiny, whirling patterns of hairs on the long, fine aristocratic nose. Stroked the head gently, the thin ears through which the sun shone, outlining veins frozen for ever. It was just like stroking a pet cat.

He sat up suddenly. A wound? If there was a wound, was this a warrior – a casualty of some star-battle brought for burial to inno-cent, bystanding Earth? A warrior buried with his weapons? For certainly the coffin was full of strange objects, packed as closely round the creature as sardines in a tin. He reached out and touched the smallest object – a red-lustre capsule like a duck-egg. He fiddled with the strange catch, sideways, up, down, and the egg broke open, the top half curling round the bottom smoothly.

Inside, a pale green substance, with a few tiny bubbles caught frozen on its surface. He sniffed it cautiously; it smelt good, some-where between cheese and peppermint. He poked the surface, leaving a fingerprint like in butter. Couldn't resist sucking his finger . . .

Wham! He shot upright. He felt so *good*. His lungs breathed deeper, sucking in air as if they had a life of their own. His heart beat faster and bigger, like a strong animal inside his ribs. A curling pleasure and warmth ran right down to his toes. His eyes . . . it was like having the very best kind of binoculars. Beetles seemed to be crawling on every blade of grass; he'd never seen so many beetles. The distant fence . . . he could follow every kink of its wire even though it was half a mile away.

And his ears! The world was a symphony of rushings and hissings and clickings and sighings, and he knew what every click and hiss was and everything was in its place.

He thought 'I am God'. Then corrected himself. 'I know how God feels . . .'

Like on Christmas morning, he plunged for the next egg. A lustrous black this time, full of blue paste. He pressed in his finger, and raised it to his lips . . .

His lips froze; no feeling. Couldn't move them. He tried to speak, shout. All that came out was a splutter of breath. The deadness crawled across his tongue, down his throat. He forgot how to breathe. He pulled his frozen, dead lips apart with his fingers; drove the bottom of his dying lungs to suck in and force out breath, while his whole face went numb and his eyes gave out and the world went black.

CHAPTER 2

He came to, lying in the heather, still trying to breathe with the shallow bottoms of his lungs. But slowly the deadly cold receded, till he could feel his fingers on his chin when he pinched it, and finally he could hear himself saying, over and over again, 'Oh no, oh no, oh no.'

He put the black egg back, wiping his fingers carefully on the heather, and ignored the other four. Lifted out the longest object instead – dull, blue-black metal. A weapon? He ran his hands over it, holding it by its various projections till it felt right. One end fitted naturally and softly into his shoulder, and a telescopic sight came up to meet his eye. 'Though he had to stretch upwards – the creature had had a longer neck.) The front edge of the handle in his right hand seemed to flex a little – a trigger? But suppose he was holding the weapon back to front? It might blow a hole in him.

He might never have fired it. He disliked killing anything. Always took a day off work when they rounded up the sheep for market, so he didn't have to see them go. The boss teased him, but turned a blind eye. No, he never would've fired it, except that five black crows flew silently across the telescopic sight. He hated crows; they picked the eyes out of new-born lambs . . .

He squeezed the trigger.

It didn't kick like a shotgun. But there was a bang that deafened him, even from far off. When he opened his eyes, not only had the crows vanished, but a huge gouge, like a railway-cutting, had been sliced out of the fellside. Bemused, he ran across. It was clean-edged, as if sliced by a knife. No explosion, no burning. As he looked, a worm came wriggling out of the sliced banking and fell into the bottom of the trench. Well, half a worm, but it still had its saddle intact; it would live. Another worm fell out, and another. Like the time he'd helped the grave-digger. He kept staring at the wound in the earth. It looked so *official*, like it had been dug by council workmen.

He walked back to the cairn, careful to keep his hand off the trigger. He didn't want his foot suddenly, surgically, vanishing. At the cairn, he turned and stared at the distant gash, still not quite able to believe he'd done it. Then he aimed at the gash and fired again. Another earth-shattering bang. But when he opened his eyes this time, the wound in the hillside had totally vanished. Everything was as it had been. Five black crows, miraculously restored, flapped their way out of the circle of the telescopic sight.

Again he ran across, wondering if he were going crazy. Not a sign of damage anywhere, not even a scorch-mark. Though there must be some very muddled worms underground . . .

He made the gully three times more; cancelled it three times more. Those worms mustn't have known whether they were coming or going. He laughed, then stopped abruptly, not liking the sound of his own laughter in that silent bowl of the fells. Finally, feeling a bit sick, and with a headache starting, he put the weapon back in its proper place.

It was then he noticed the helmets. Two, side by side, above the creature's head. One was matt black, and seemed to repel the light and lurk in its own shadow. It was dented, the visor scorched. Something told him it was a war-helmet; he pulled his hand back, sick of weapons.

The other, though, had to be peaceful. It glittered with patterns, red and gold and blue, arranged in playful shapes that seemed to move under his eye. Somehow he knew it had to be a fun-helmet. He picked it up, and put it on. It was far too big for him; built to accommodate the creature's huge ears. But as he pulled the visor down over his eyes, he felt little thin gentle things, like cats' whiskers, reach out from the inside of the helmet and touch his ears, eyes, start growing up his nostrils and into his mouth. He cried out and tried to snatch the helmet off.

Too late; he was already in a different place.

Darkness. Then a door swung up, and metal steps swung out beneath his feet. And he was staring down at hundreds of the creatures, black or grey, striped or spotted. They stared up at him, upright, still and silent, so he should have been afraid. Except that their eyes were like the warm, blinking eyes of a cat sitting by the fire, and the air was filled with a profound, soft purring that soothed him.

He stepped out on to the steps. Immediately, every right paw was raised in silent salute; long, furry fingers, claws retracted; black pads on the palm. He saw the blur of his own right arm shooting up in response, round the edge of his helmet. And there was striped fur on it. And they opened their mouths and whispered, and a sound like 'Prepoc' came out.

'Prepoc! Prepoc! Prepoc!' They breathed it with wonder, and he knew it was his name. Then he walked down the yellow metal steps, soundlessly, as if he was walking on fur. And he was among them, and they were pressing in on him, rubbing softly against every part of him and there was no aloneness any more, no cold, no fear, no hunger. 'Prepoc! Prepoc! Prepoc!'

At last it ended, and they were gone, their purring fading down the wind. Only one lone creature remained, and he knew with a stir in his body that she was female and he knew her. Then there were three more of them, striped females, nearly grown and all exactly alike. Then four more males, scarcely half-grown, and all exactly alike.

And then they all ran, together, under an orange sky with twin suns, under great, craggy cliffs, across tumbled fields of boulders, warm under his feet in the light of the twin suns. And it was a delight to stiff and weary muscles to leap and climb, to fall and twist and land sure-footed without pain.

Eventually, the joy ended. It was dusk, and all around him yellow fighting-ships were climbing into the air on thunderous flame, and hovering.

Waiting for him. And again, the great assembly of creatures pressed in round him. Only there was no purring, but great sadness now. And he climbed the metal steps, and they raised their black paws, and the steps were drawn in and the door shut and there was darkness.

Then the helmet retracted its little whiskers from his ears and eyes, from up inside his nostrils and from out of his mouth, and he reached up and raised the visor, and he was sitting on the fell and the clouds were massing heavy. On his hand he felt the first spot of rain.

He pulled off the helmet, and realized it was a memory-helmet; a bit like the family snapshots that every soldier carries around in his wallet. But he was glad; I'm glad you made it home, Prepoc, warrior, hero, leader.

Then he saw Prepoc lying on the open fellside, with the first drops of earth-rain making dark patches on his fur.

He put the helmet back, and got the coffin-lid closed quickly. The rain came down in torrents, soaking him, making his hands slip on the stones as he carefully rebuilt the cairn, which glistened dully in the green rain-light.

Then he raised his right arm in the same salute, and turned wearily for home. The dogs were waiting as he crossed the crest and home came in sight, far down the valley. The dogs were soaked, miserable, slinking tail-down through the downpour, but Ralph walked feeling like a god. Nobody else on earth knew what he knew. Prepoc, hero, Prepoc my friend, dead among the stars yet here on earth to touch. He'd never tell a soul . . .

He stopped feeling godlike the moment he walked through the back door.

'Where you been? You've had me worried sick. What time's this supposed to be? Your tea's been in the oven two hours – all dried up and serve you right. *And* it was sausage and chips,' added Mam with satisfaction, this being Ralph's favourite meal.

'I thought you'd gone down some bog-hole in the fell and we'd never find you. I was just going to go an' ring the poliss . . . an' just look at you . . . look at your anorak . . . anoraks don't grow on trees you know . . . fourteen pound that cost me in Penrith market and now look at it. What you been doing . . . rebuilding the M6? . . . and Mr Norton's been down looking for the dogs and I didn't know what to say to him. You're more bother now than you were when you were little you worry me sick and you're nearly eighteen get those filthy soaking clothes off this instant before you catch your death . . .' Mam stopped to draw a big breath.

'Aw Mam . . .'

'Get them off I say.' Big as he was, she was bigger, tall and raw-boned in her faded, flowered pinny. She grabbed his anorak and ripped down the zip, and peeled him out of it with an energy that spun him clean round the kitchen. 'And your trousers . . .' She was kneeling at his feet now, undoing the laces of his boots. 'And look at these . . . these won't be dry by the morning, no matter how much paper I stuff in them. And look at the toes all scuffed, not two months old and they won't last two months more. I told you not to buy that Polish rubbish. D'you think we're made of money?' She hauled off one boot, nearly sending him crashing to the floor, and started on the other, while he hung on desperately to the high mantelpiece. 'Now let's have those trousers – you could wring them out like dishcloths.' One yank and they were down, leaving his legs all pale, damp and goosepimply. 'And get that jumper off, and that shirt. It's not now you'll feel it, when you're young and daft. It's when you're a grown man wi' a wife an' kids to support, an' you can't move wi' rheumatism. You'll thank me then.'

He gave up and let her haul the sweater violently up over his head, scrawping his face painfully with the hard wet wool. But he drew the line with his underpants, fighting desperately for his dignity.

'Oh, catch your death – see if I care.' She picked up the big brown blanket, from where it had been warming over the fireguard ready, and threw it in his face. 'Your dad was crippled wi' rheumatics, long afore he died.' She reached for the old black kettle simmering on the stove, and shoved him into the rocker, by the fire that she kept burning even in the desolate heat of summer. He snuggled into the warmth of the blanket, making sure that no piece of his damp white skin was exposed. The rough warmth of the blanket was a comfort he'd known all his life. Getting wet, having toothache, flu, the hot blanket had seen him through everything. He listened to her rattling the kettle, a glass and a spoon violently on the old, worn kitchen table. The sharp smells of lemon and whisky came subtly to his nose; her voice was softening slightly, as her first rage passed; became almost soothing, like the sound of the sea breaking over him. It was slowly becoming somebody else's fault.

'Jack Norton has no right to keep you up't fell in this sort o' weather, idle old sod, while he's laikin' in't kitchen. He's just like his father . . . always had money the Nortons . . . never sweated in their lives.' She thrust the steaming glass of lemon and whisky into his hands. 'Get that down yer, then straight for your bath. I'll run it.' He caught his breath as the whisky spilled red-hot on to his bare legs, then inhaled deeply of the smell, listening to her stamp upstairs and across the creaking ceiling overhead. Heard the plug plonk in the

19

plughole and the water start running. He sipped gently, so the whisky wouldn't scald his lips, and hugged the secret of Prepoc to him closer than the blanket. Then she was back.

'C'mon. Bathwater's gettin' cold.'

'Aw Mam, I haven't finished me whisky . . .'

Her hand descended on his ear, stingingly. He clung to the glass, but more scalding liquid hit his bare legs through the blanket, making him wince. 'I told you to drink it while it was hot. Won't do you no good otherwise. I can't do wi' you dreaming by the fire all day. Jack Norton can afford it – we can't.'

Muttering, wrapped in the blanket like an Indian squaw, he creaked upstairs. The bathwater was scalding too; he ran in some cold surreptitiously, hoping she wouldn't hear and knock on the ceiling with her broom-handle. But she was too busy. He heard the washing-machine being dragged across the stone flags of the kitchen floor; her god, her pride and joy. And all the time she was rumbling on, like a storm blowing itself out. He wondered who she thought she was talking to – the washing-machine, himself, Jack Norton, his long-dead father, or merely herself, keeping the cruel, unfeeling, treacherous world at bay with a storm of words?

He lowered himself into the bath with a sigh of luxury, as the washing-machine began thumping downstairs. He didn't bother soaping himself – he'd only had his official bath the day before – but just lay dreamily, looking at his pink feet sticking out of the water like twin Rocks of Gibraltar, so far away; feeling the sting as the soap-powder she'd put in the water worked its way into little cuts and grazes he'd never realized he'd got, rebuilding the cairn. Stared at the cracks in the bathroom ceiling; at the patch on the bath his mother had rubbed bare and grey with scouring-powder; at the flowered wallpaper she'd stuck on with her own hands . . . a piece had lifted with the steam and was curling up like a butterfly's wing. Mam would flatten that the moment she saw it. The night darkened the pebbled glass of the bathroom window. The washing-machine thumped on downstairs.

And then he thought he heard another noise, beyond the hiss of the refilling cold-water tank, the thumping of the washing-machine and his mother's murmuring. A noise far above him, he thought, up in the sky, coming and going, teasing his ear, playing hide-and-seek with him, but coming nearer.

Helicopter? Oh, not again! This district was plagued with mysterious helicopters, flying by night with or without lights, in the strangest directions and with no purpose at all. Every three months or so, somebody would write to the local paper about it. There'd be a real outburst of letters, then the editor would write a stinging editorial. The county police, consulted, would admit themselves baffled, or blame army manoeuvres. Once, an inspector on the telly had bent his elbow with a knowing grin, implying it was only drunken yokels on their way home from the pub; he'd been severely reprimanded. In the pub they blamed sheep-stealers, international drug-rings, flying saucers. Most sensible people reckoned it was the government and *we'd* never get to know anything about it. There'd been noisy debates about how many sheep you could get in a helicopter. This helicopter would pass, like all the rest.

But it didn't. It got closer; seemed to be hanging right over the house . . . the feeling was strong enough to get Ralph out of the bath, trying to stare upwards out of the bathroom window. But all he got was the night air cooling his hot, wet skin . . . if it *was* up there, it was out of sight beyond the gable and the chimneys.

Then he got a funny feeling; as if the air was silently falling apart; as if the inside of his head was going hollow. He thrust his fingers into his ears and wiggled them vigorously, thinking some water must have got into them. None had; yet the queer, hollow feeling in his head got stronger and stronger.

Suddenly frightened, he wiggled his ears again. Was he going to have a fit, like Billy Hargreaves at school? Or drop down dead of a stroke, like old Mrs Riley at the Harvest Supper, laughing one minute and dead the next, with blood running out of her pale, pale nose? He stared around at the familiar bathroom for help, at the bathmat with the raggy edge, the cracked block of yellow soap that seemed to have been there ever since he could remember. But they were no help; the feeling in his head was shutting him off from them, was sending him down into some frightening hell . . . he tried to yell 'Mam' but his voice wouldn't work.

Then he heard the washing-machine stop thumping; heard his mother turn the knob and send the filthy scalding water down the new sewage-pipe they were all still so proud of; like a little scalding underground stream, leaping down to the new sewage-works by the River Eden.

Immediately, the feeling in his head stopped; became an absurd nothing, as if it had never been; it *must* have been water in his

21

ears ... In his relief, he played the game he always played on these occasions, pulling the plug in the bath and sending his own hot, dirty water down to join his mother's, increasing the flow running so fast underground.

There was a sudden subtle change in the noise above the house; a moving away of the disturbance in the air. As if the helicopter had turned its attention elsewhere; was chasing the swift-moving stream of boiling water underground ...

He smiled, told himself not to be silly.

At that moment, there was a terrifying crash. From quite a long way off. Just one; short, sharp, cut off. Then he could hear its echoes, rumbling along the fellside. The bathroom window shuddered, in its wooden frame. Little pieces of whitewash floated down from the ceiling.

Then silence. Then dogs barking, hens cackling up at the farm. Then men shouting. He ran out of the bathroom naked, as Mam yelled 'Ralph!' up the stairs, like it was all *his* fault. He ran into his bedroom and threw on the first shirt and trousers he could lay his hands on. Ran outside, his shoelaces flicking round his feet.

The little street was full of men with torches, and women huddled in groups, cuddling themselves. Everybody shouting.

'It's the Atomic blown up, over at Sellafield ...'

'No, it were nearer, just outside t' village ...'

'Down by't river ...'

'Like them bombs Jerry dropped at Ravenglass, in't war.'

'I heard t'same sound eight times today,' said a vague shadow. 'But it were further off, way up on't fell ... thowt they were blasting in the old lead-mines. T'government ...'

Fear squeezed Ralph's heart for the second time that night.

This bang *had* been the same as Prepoc's blaster had made. He realized that now. His legs began to shake; he heard himself panting; he bent down to tie his shoelaces, to hide his terror. What had he done? What had he started, up there on the fell? Suppose Prepoc hadn't been dead, merely asleep? Suppose he'd wakened him ...

'It were down towards the sewage-farm, I swear,' said somebody. Slowly they all began to move in the direction of the river, men hopping over the stone walls, women grumbling, going round by the gates. Ralph didn't want to go, didn't want to see what had happened. But he was afraid of being left alone. Suddenly he was far from sure that Prepoc was his friend, or anybody else's. He really didn't know anything about Prepoc at all. Prepoc dead was one thing; Prepoc alive, stalking through the dark, was another. He kept close to Mam, in the middle of the crowd of women. Mam was blaming the Tories; it was like that government pumping-station that blew up, killing all those parish councillors in the Lake District. Ralph knew she was wrong; that she hadn't a clue. And yet he clung to her; he'd rather believe in Mam than believe in Prepoc awake. Prepoc awake was the kind of nightmare that Mam had always sent away, simply by being Mam.

It wasn't easy in the dark, even with torches. Ralph stumbled along, hanging on to the endless sound of Mam's voice, and praying to Somebody that none of it had really ever happened and vowing that if the Somebody made it not happen, he'd never go near that cairn again . . .

Then one man was coming back, shouting.

'The buggers have blown up the sewage-works. Bloody I R A musta done it. It's *gone*,' his voice rose to an incredulous shriek. 'Clean as a whistle.'

They gathered, slowly, round where their little sewage-works had been. Just a round concrete tank, with the circling pipes that sprayed the sewage, and the little flat-topped concrete hut with ventilators, that held the machinery. All gone, as the man had said, clean as a whistle. And the earth scooped out beneath it in a deep hole, into which the sewage was starting to run from the severed end of the pipe, with a vile soapy smell.

'A bomb . . . I R A . . . the bastards.'

'Steady on, Jack. Mebbe it's just a methane-gas explosion – lots of methane gas in sewers.'

'But . . . but . . .' said one man, 'there's no *wreckage*. No broken bricks. Just gone, clean as a whistle.' A forest of torch-beams played round the sheer, clean sides of the hole. It looked so . . . official . . . like a hole that had been dug by council workmen. As Ralph watched, a worm, a half-worm, wriggled out of the clear-cut edge, and fell with a plop into the growing pool of evil-smelling sewage.

'I don't get it,' said the man.

Ralph did.

CHAPTER 3

They straggled back towards the village, the men still arguing, the women starting to wonder what to get for supper. Until they reached the first cottage . . .

The second explosion hit them like a wave that hurt their ears, coming from behind. It rolled over them, and banged back an echo from the stone walls of the cottages.

'They've done it again!'

'My God, what've they blown up now?'

'Nowhere's safe . . .'

The tall, well-built figure of Jack Norton, in his cap, long droopy raincoat and wellies, broke into a gallop. 'I'll phone the police.'

Like one man, picking up the smaller children, the villagers ran after him. Children caught their parents' panic and began to cry. One elderly woman fell over, hurt her hands and knees, and was picked up and dragged along sobbing wildly. Suddenly, people were not outraged, but terrified. They began pushing each other, up the narrow lane to Jack's house, panicking like a flock of sheep with a killer-dog after it. Jack's back door banged back against his passage wall with a sickening crack, and banged again and again, as people fought to get in. Ralph heard something tip over: a large piece of china had smashed on the floor. Then he was swept into Norton's kitchen, where Jack was desperately trying to look up the number of the Penrith police station in a big telephone directory which kept slipping out of his hands, while he screamed at his wife to find his reading spectacles.

'Nine-nine-nine,' shouted everybody. 'Nine-nine-nine!' But Jack was deaf as well as blind. People tried to grab the phone away from him. He pulled the handset back against his chest desperately, and the whole phone, and the spindly table it sat on, fell to the floor among the trampling feet . . .

God knows how it would have ended, if Denis Button hadn't taken charge. Denis, now demobbed, had been a para in the Falklands.

Possibly the most stupid para in the Falklands. People said snidly that they wondered, with Denis there, how we'd won at all. Since his demob, he'd worn his green para pullover, with the patches at elbow and shoulder, day and night. He'd even tried to wear it at his brother's wedding, till his Mam stopped him and got him into his good suit. And all his talk was of Argies, till they called him Argie Button behind his back. But not to his face, because he was a big lad, and inclined to be nasty when roused.

Now a great light dawned on his face; his finest hour had come. Now he could show them how he'd earned his single stripe; Goose Green would live again, even if Denis had been guarding lorries at base camp at the time . . .

'Fire and movement,' he shouted. 'Fire and movement!'

It was such a totally inappropriate thing to shout that he silenced everybody. And while they were all gaping, and even the little kids had stopped crying, tears drying on their amazed faces, he added:

'Getcher shotguns!'

That they understood. Every man in the village had a shotgun; rabbits helped to fill the pot on a farmhand's wages. The men ran for their guns; the kitchen half emptied. Mrs Norton said 'I'll brew some tea.' Another woman said 'First-aid kit!' and ran home to fetch hers. 'Hot soup' said another and ran to get her tins. Suddenly, everyone had thought of something useful to do. Children were removed forcibly to the farm parlour, cold with the memory of funerals and vicars' visits; hung with pictures of Roman lovers chastely entwined and the uncomfortable, samplered motto 'Thou God Seest Me'. Jack Norton, scrabbling on his knees with his useless spectacles halfway down his nose, recovered the telephone, clutched it to his chest, and was finally persuaded to dial '999'.

Ralph ran after the men: burst into Mam's kitchen and, by the light of the dying fire, grabbed up Dad's old shotgun from the corner, where it had been gathering dust for fifteen years. He had no ammo, but he ran back into the street. Any minute Prepoc might appear, a shambling, half-dead thing driven insane by waking, after the sleep of centuries, into a world where he understood nothing. Or would he be calm and deadly in his black fighting-helmet, wanting revenge for that dreadful impiety on the fell? Ralph did not know which he dreaded most . . .

Denis Button, however, had no such doubts. Denis was fighting the IRA. A stream of strange phrases continued to issue from his mouth. Not just 'Fire and movement' over and over again, but 'Dead ground' and 'Field of fire' and 'Section-leaders to me!' It didn't matter. The men were having ideas of their own, an ancient Home Guard among them. The roads and alleys leading into the village were being blocked by backing and turning Landrovers, and chugging, snorting tractors. Upstairs-windows were being shoved open, or, if unopenable, broken out with shotgun barrels. Men were settling behind the high stone walls, staring out into the darkness across suddenly threatening fields they had known all their lives. Some shotguns rattled gently and metallically against the tops of the walls, as the hands that held them shook.

'Jerry can come as soon as he likes,' quavered the ancient Home Guard. 'We're ready for him.' And they were as ready as any hamlet of twenty houses and thirty shotguns could be.

'Got any cartridges, son?' asked old Togger Smurthwaite, as Ralph edged alongside him.

'No.'

'Here's four – I've got two whole boxes.'

The fat shells comforted Ralph. He shoved two in his pocket, broke the shotgun and pushed the other two home.

'Putcher safety-catch on,' said Togger quietly. 'If you've got one.' Then 'I've always wanted a crack at them IRA bastards . . .' He said it so quietly, he might have been talking about foxes.

Only Ralph knew it wasn't the IRA, or foxes. He knew he was going to have to kill Prepoc, if he could. Suppose Prepoc came lurching across the fields now, into the headlights of the Landrovers . . . would the men shoot at him, without realizing what he was? Or would they run away in terror, leaving Ralph alone with him? Or would a sudden burst of Prepoc's blaster blow them all clean out of life between one breath and another, as it had the sewage-farm?

If he was left alone with Prepoc, should he try to say he was sorry? Say 'Punish me – the rest are innocent'? But how *could* Prepoc understand? Ralph would have to put him down, put him out of his misery . . .

The tears running down his face didn't bother him much; it was dark and nobody could see. But then his rotten body, beyond his control, began to gasp and snort. And he felt Togger notice and stiffen. Now Togger would think he was a coward, and he *wasn't* a coward . . .

There came a sound of women's voices from behind them, and the sound of china clinking.

'Tea's up,' said Togger gently. 'Gotter match son? Came out wi'out mine. I could do wi' a smoke. How about you?'

'No smoking,' shouted Argie Button. 'Snipers.'

They stood drinking tea; and went on peering out over the quiet fields.

The police Panda ignored the shouted challenges, and nearly got a barrage of shotgun-pellets through its windscreen for its pains. It pulled up with a screech of brakes, just two inches short of the tractor-barrier.

'Christ,' said the familiar voice of Sergeant Dudley, 'I think I'll give up rural bobbying. I think I'll get a transfer to Chicago, for a rest. What the hell is going on?'

Twenty voices tried to tell him; and the radio in the car kept drawing him back inside. But his official voice calmed them. He talked about 'incidents' and gave precise times like twenty-one fifteen. 'Army's on its way from Carlisle,' he said; and it got a cheer, like the raising of the Siege of Mafeking. Then he took Jack Norton into the Panda, and made them move the tractors, and drove on towards the sewage-farm, round by the road. Then they put the tractors back across the street-ends and the women brought round hot soup, and Togger went off into a dark corner and made a noise among the nettles like Niagara Falls, explaining his bladder wasn't what it used to be.

Then the Panda came back, and a very angry Sergeant Dudley was getting out. This time it was his turn to be incoherent. The whole village gathered round, but all they could make out was obscenities.

Jack Norton got out the other side. 'It's come back,' he said with a bleat. 'The sewage-works has come back. Just where it ought to be. Working,' he added. 'Working like a sewing-machine.'

Behind him, over the radio, Sergeant Dudley turned back the Army Bomb Squad, still on the road from Carlisle. The villagers listened stupefied as he cancelled police reinforcements, dog-handlers, personnel-carriers . . . while Jack Norton went on bleating 'It's still there. Working like a sewing-machine' with the monotony of a talking parrot.

'I suppose I should send for Social Services,' said the sergeant finally, to the assembled crowd, 'but you can't put a whole village in the loony-bin.'

27

Then he drove away and left them.

Slowly, timidly, the men still carrying their shotguns and Togger calling out for everybody to unload, the village straggled across the fields towards the sewage-farm. There was a mist down, floating just overhead, cutting the tops off the trees. Somewhere above, the moon came out, filling the sky with a vague, milky glow.

Only Ralph didn't unload; only Ralph was still terrified, expecting any moment to see the stark, upright shape of Prepoc come stalking vengefully out of the mist towards them.

But they reached the sewage-farm without incident. And there it was indeed, working as silently and sweetly as a sewing-machine, the sprinkler-arm circling slowly, dripping a cascade of jewelled droplets on to the sewage.

'I'm giving up drink,' said Jack Norton.

'I haven't had a drop all night, and *I* saw it,' said his wife.

'Bit smelly,' said somebody. 'An' the ground's soggy. Must be leaking.'

'If it had just been *leaking*,' said Jack Norton, 'I'd've rung up the Water Board.'

'Let's write to the papers,' said Togger. 'There might be the price of a drink in it.'

Slowly, relief descended on Ralph. Wherever Prepoc was now, whatever he was doing, he wasn't *insane*; he wasn't a crazy, shambling Frankenstein monster. He'd taken away the sewage-farm for some mysterious purpose of his own; then put it back unharmed. He hadn't killed anybody; he wasn't running amok. If he punishes me, thought Ralph, I deserve it. So he took the shells out of his shotgun.

He walked beside Mam, amazed at the things people were saying. They were going on about flying saucers and the mystery of the *Marie Celeste* and the Bermuda triangle. They were turning what had happened into just another queer article in *Unexplained* magazine. They were oddly happy, as if something wonderful had happened to them, like winning the pools. I mean, thought Ralph, something was clearly taken away, then brought back, against all the laws of nature; and they were just wearing away the *incredibleness* of it by talking about it. Within weeks, they'd have cut it down to 'that funny do at Unthank'. Willingly blinding themselves to the truth, like ostriches burying their heads in the sand. Were all adults this mad?

But he noticed how quick they were to say goodnight and get inside their houses; and he heard them turning the keys in their back doors, something they never did normally.

CHAPTER 4

They wrote to the papers. The papers sent reporters; the reporters listened sympathetically, till the words 'sewage-farm' were mentioned. Then they pressed their lips together, swiftly drank up their tea, and departed. Nothing appeared in the papers, even though it was the silly season when headlines appeared like: 'HOUSEWIFE GAVE GOLDFISH THE KISS OF LIFE'...

The only result was that when the villagers met people from other villages at Penrith on market-day, there were unhelpful inquiries about the consumption of peas and exploding toilets and Martians getting out of flying saucers and asking to use the loo. The village was referred to as 'Shitville'. Several fist-fights took place in the backyards of pubs, and three of the village men were later fined heavily for causing an affray. But as Togger Smurthwaite said grimly, stroking his knuckles, it was worth it.

After that, the story did get into the papers, about this village that had suffered some kind of mass-hallucination, and the village nickname was changed to Pottyville, which it has remained to the present day.

But Ralph noticed how life in the village had changed. People *huddled*. Men huddled together at their work; the farmers cut their silage early, and worked in gangs to get each other's in. And you always carried shotguns when you were out cutting silage; in case you got a pot at a rabbit...

When they weren't cutting silage, they were mending fences or cleaning out pigsties, close to home. Nobody seemed to want to work on his own, out in the farther fields.

In the evenings, all the men went to the pub; even Ralph, which was something unheard-of. One morning, while he was dressing, he heard Mam out in the lane, tackling the pub-landlord about it.

'I wouldn't worry, Mrs Edwards,' said the landlord nervously. 'We won't make an alcoholic out of him. He just sits there, making a half-pint shandy last all night. He's getting a dab-hand at dominoes, though!'

'Wickedness,' said Mam, like a cat spitting. But it seemed to lack some of her usual spirit. Like all the women, she tended to join others, drinking tea and knitting in a house where there were young children, while the men were at the pub. Nobody wanted to be alone after dark.

Ralph enjoyed the pub. He sat in the snug with the older men, playing dominoes, with all the sheepdogs sitting under the tables beside their owners, and occasionally snapping at strangers' ankles if they moved their feet carelessly. Sporadic dogfights under the tables were put down with vicious slapping of suddenly doffed caps. Ralph preferred dominoes and listening to talk of the old days, rather than mixing with the younger lot in the public bar, where Johnny Sligo was always shooting his mouth off, or playing the same out-of-date record on the juke-box, over and over again.

After nothing else odd had happened for a fortnight, the men took to going out in groups just before dusk, with their shotguns, saying they were going to pot rabbits. Of course, people had always gone potting rabbits at dusk, but not in groups of five or six; it was a hard time for the bunnies. Ralph thought that what they were really doing was beating the bounds, or like an army, sending out patrols. But they just talked as if their only interest was potting rabbits.

And during the day, Ralph saw a remarkable number of people walking in twos and threes down to the sewage-farm, or coming back from it. He followed one or two to find out what they were doing. But they just stood staring for about ten minutes, then came home without saying much. Except how the smell of the spilt sewage still lingered, and how long and rank the grass was growing . . .

Another week passed, and still nothing. Except a calf with two heads was born at Askrigg, and the curate at Threlkeld ran off with the churchwarden's wife. One glorious evening, Ralph stood a long time at his gate, wondering whether to go down to the pub. He was sick of dominoes, and holding his feet still under the table so the dogs didn't bite him. It was a marvellous soft warm evening. Westwards, the sun was setting over the distant mountains of the Lake District, making them purple-edged and sharp (a sure sign of rain before morning). Eastwards, the sun lit the bracken of the fell to a pure gold, and winked on the windscreens of the cars and lorries as they twisted and turned, climbing Hartside Height. It was an evening on

31

which nothing bad could possibly happen . . . Ralph felt like going for a walk.

Up towards the cairn? The thought slid into his mind like a black, exciting temptation, making his belly crawl with excitement. *Dare* he? Well, if he only went a little way . . . took the dogs to warn him . . . took the shotgun . . .

He met Jack Norton, as he picked up the dogs.

'What's t' gun for, lad?'

'Rabbits,' said Ralph, shortly.

'Eeh, thee'rt changin'. Happen tha Mam will be glad on a rabbit.'

If he only knew . . .

The first part of the climb up the green-road wasn't frightening. He had the dogs circling ahead; they'd bark to warn him. Their ears and noses were ten times better than his . . .

Then one of them did bark; the bark that meant strangers. He had the shells in the shotgun before he knew.

But it was only holiday-makers; a boy and a girl coming down the green-road, hand in hand. As he spotted them, they stopped and embraced passionately. Ralph had an idea it was done for his benefit. He didn't realize he was glowering so grimly till the boy said nervously, in a Brummie accent:

'We're not trespassing . . .'

'No,' said Ralph. 'Not here on the green-road. Have you seen anything funny up there?'

'Like what?' asked the boy, and the girl giggled.

'Dead sheep.' The girl gave a daft little scream.

'No – no dead sheep. Is there a killer-dog on the loose?' Ralph knew he was taking the piss; he walked on in a black fury. Before he'd gone ten yards, they were giggling behind his back.

His fury carried him on, recklessly, to where the green-road met the main road winding up Hartside Height – the place where he normally left the scrambler. He stood watching the evening traffic stream past, a dog on each side of him. A tripper-bus passed, and a row of girls on the back seat waved and whistled. Irrationally, they took away nearly all his fear. He suddenly decided to walk on up to the cairn . . .

And still he felt almost safe, as he climbed sweating up the tussocks. This was *his* fell; nobody knew it like him. And the sheep were acting normally; the small flocks were fleeing *away* from him; nothing but him and the dogs were frightening them. Nothing scary could possibly be lurking over the next rise . . . the lapwings were resting normally, where they always rested at this time of year. The curlew were calling from their hidden feeding-places, just as they always did. He knew with his whole body that there was nothing alien loose on the fell.

But as he approached the cairn, he still circled it widely, absurdly cautious in case something might be lurking behind. It looked whole and undisturbed but . . .

The dogs had no such fears. They raced up to it. Nance leapt up on top, silhouetting herself imposingly against the sky, ears pricked, monarch of all she surveyed. Jet cocked up one leg against it . . . Ralph moved in, laughing at his own fears, and yet . . . a little disappointed.

Yes, the stones of the cairn were still piled as he had left them . . . he knew his own careful handiwork . . . then, ridiculously, he began to doubt they were his own handiwork. Better just take a quick peep.

It wasn't until he had uncovered the coffin that he realized its three clips couldn't have been undone from the inside; no more than the clips of a suitcase could be. And they were still closed; nothing had burst them open. So he opened them himself, sending the dogs away fleeing, snarling. Lifted the lid with a wildly beating heart.

Prepoc lay as Ralph had left him. There was conclusive proof; one tuft of his fur lay awry, curled over by the butt of the blaster, carelessly replaced when Ralph had been racing against the storm. *Prepoc had never moved.* And Ralph knew he never would move. He was dead, dead as the mummified cat in the British Museum. Maybe dead as long as the cat in the British Museum. He had never gone beserk; never wrecked the sewage-farm . . .

'Sorry, Prepoc,' said Ralph, smoothing down the fur where the butt of the blaster had disturbed it, glad that Prepoc was still his secret, still his friend.

He piled the stones carefully back, relieved and yet a little . . . flat. It wasn't until he'd replaced the last stone that the thought hit him.

If it hadn't been Prepoc at the sewage-farm . . .

Who?

It wasn't Prepoc up here on the fell he had to worry about. It was something down in the valley.

Something between him and home.

And the sun was just dipping behind the Lakeland hills, sending the long shadows of the cairn and the dogs, of himself, stretching across the tussocks and the heather.

In twenty minutes, it would be dark.

He ran all the way, panting and slavering, stumbling in the dusk, carrying the loaded gun. It was a wonder he didn't shoot his foot off . . .

He had to walk round the village a long time before his breath quietened enough for him to dive into the pub.

CHAPTER 5

The next thing . . . at first Ralph wasn't sure whether it was anything at all. He was walking past the farmhouse door two nights later, going home, when Mrs Norton called him in.

'Canst tha do cows tonight, Ralph? This un reckons his back's bad again!'

Jack Norton lay full length on the kitchen settle, his mucky wellies still on his feet, their soles displaying straw and dung to eye and nose. He raised himself on one elbow, then fell back with a heartfelt groan. 'I'm badly tonight, Ralph! There was never a farmer over forty didn't ha' a bad back. Shoulda taken that soft office job like me Dad said.'

Mrs Norton sniffed audibly. There was a smell of beer as well as dung, and an empty pint glass on the stone slabs under the settle. But Ralph didn't mind. Tea was never till half past six, on the dot, every night; and Mam could use the extra overtime-money. Besides, he liked cows. He yelled for Jet and Nance, and set off up the road.

The cows were waiting round the gate, lowing urgently, their udders painfully swollen; they should've been milked by four o'clock. It was a good job Jack Norton had his Dad's money; he'd never have made a living as a farmer. Ralph opened the gate, and the cows started down the lane for the milking-parlour, eager as commuters for their train. Jet and Nance snapped at the last cow's heel, making her break into an ungainly ten-yard gallop. They were allowed to nip cows, and enjoyed it hugely; it would have meant their deaths to bite sheep. Still, they'd curdle the milk if they galloped the cows too much . . . Ralph picked up a clod of earth and threw it warningly at them. The clod burst under their tails, showering them with fine pellets of earth. They looked back slyly, and desisted.

The journey wasn't so peaceful as to be boring. Cows had their funny little ways, and their peck-order. They knew who was allowed to walk in front of who; rule-breakers were butted up their backsides and sometimes a fight broke out. Sometimes they mounted

35

each other, in poor imitation of bulls . . . something to do with one cow dominating another. Or they stuck their necks through into neighbours' fields, for a quick chew at the greener grass, and sometimes got their heads stuck. Ralph thought how like people they were, every one different. There was the rotten old bitch that tried to stand on your foot in the milking-parlour, when she thought you weren't looking. She weighed about half a ton, so it was quite an experience, even if your boots did have steel toecaps. There was the old bitch who tried to crush you against the side of the stall with her belly; till you gave her a sharp kick on the hock. There was even the one who once idly turned and bit through the wing of a waiting car. Cost Jack Norton a bit, she did.

You had to keep them moving . . .

And, a hundred yards ahead, they were *not* moving. The front ones had stopped, and the ones behind were piling up . . . damn! Was it some fool in a car, trying to force his way through the herd? Ralph stepped to one side, on to the grass verge, and peered, trying to make out what was happening. There didn't seem to be a car . . . must be a fight. Soon break that up!

'Ga on, Jet! Ga on, Nance!'

Authorized to nip cow-heels, the dogs swept off, barking joyfully. But the jam of cows did not break up. In fact, the back ones were swinging round in the lane clumsily, tails lashing the hawthorn hedge, and coming back towards him. The dogs barking rose to a frantic crescendo, as they tried to stem the tide. Then their barks turned to surprised yelps as the cows ran them down, sending them sprawling in the strawy dust of the road. Now the whole herd was past the dogs, coming at Ralph in a gallop . . .

Luckily, he kept his head. He didn't just stand and let them run past; he ran back to the open gate of the field they'd just left, and stood blocking the road beyond it, arms and stick outstretched, making himself look twice the size, twice as frightening.

He didn't think they would turn in time; he thought he was going to be flattened. But habit is strong in cows; one turned into the field, the rest followed, and he shut the gate on them, panting hard. That herd weighed forty tons, and cost forty thousand pounds!

Then he turned to swear at the dogs, for their incompetence.

The dogs weren't there. Way down the road, he could hear their hysterical barking. Something had really got them going . . . had they cornered a fox? But a fox wouldn't stand long enough to get

36

them really frantic. Was it a killer-dog from the town? Some wild animal escaped from a zoo? He ran towards them, clutching his stick tight and wishing it was bigger and heavier.

They were crouched in the middle of the road, very close together, staring at the right-hand hedge. Their tails were plumed; the hackles on their backs standing up more than they had for the body of Prepoc, up on the fell. And they were slowly backing away, slinking down on their haunches. Their wild barks were losing force and confidence . . . turning into yelps.

They were giving in to something . . .

He called, to let them know he was coming. 'Stay, Jet! Stay, Nance!'

They turned and ran to him . . .

Then ran straight past without stopping, tails between their legs, beaten.

He was alone, with whatever it was behind the right-hand hedge. He brandished his stick, held it out in front of him, to give himself courage. Was it a rabid dog? That had to happen some time, however careful the government was . . . he'd have to ram his stick down the foaming jaws and fend it off somehow . . . he advanced. Whatever had frightened the dogs was behind a gap in the hedge, which had been filled in by a few sticks of fence. The hedge hadn't been cut for a bit; it stuck too far out into the lane, blocking his view so he couldn't see a thing.

He took two more hesitant steps; and then he saw it. The setting sun was behind it. It stood, a black shape, taller than a man. Two huge, pricked ears . . .

Then he made a noise in his throat that was half relief, and half rage. It was only a huge black Alsatian dog, standing up with its paws on top of the fence. It was wearing a collar, and some kind of name-medallion hung from that collar. Somebody's spoiled pet, got loose; must belong to some townie holiday-maker. Well, they'd better come and take it home quick before somebody shot it. Worrying cows like that! Enough to give a cow in-calf a miscarriage. Dogs had been shot for less than that round here, before now. He waved his stick angrily at it, swore at it, expecting it to run away.

It didn't move. He was shocked by the thickness of its hairy black body; it must be heavier than he was. He was shocked by the size of its head, of its jaws, of the teeth each side of that lolling red tongue. But it was the eyes that frightened him most. He judged dogs by their eyes ... the warm, intelligent, near-human eyes of collies ... the melting, mournful, please-love-me eyes of spaniels ... the sly, flicking eyes of a dog that's been hit too much ... the set, marble-like eyes of a dog that's going to bite you ... it was none of these. It had ... arrogant eyes ... inspecting him ... it thinks it's as good as I am. I'll be damned if I'm going to be outfaced by a dog.

But Ralph's eyes dropped first ...

He made himself stare at the dog again ... it certainly wasn't rabid ... it looked in perfect glossy health ... its eyes were still staring at him, cool, assessing. He stepped nearer, shook his stick within inches of its face.

It still did not move. Ralph grew afraid. Sweat began to run down his back, under his shirt. There was something very queer about this dog, but he couldn't work out what it was. Except a thing as big as that, that wasn't afraid of a man ... shouldn't be allowed to live ... it should be *shot*.

What could he do? His stick, held before him, began to shake and waver. He began to whimper to himself ... if he ran away it might attack ...

There was a blast of a car-horn behind him, that made him jump a foot in the air. He spun round, and saw it was the police Panda, with Sergeant Dudley sitting at the wheel, grimacing at him, and waving him aside.

He looked back at the gap in the hedge; the dog was gone. He gestured helplessly at the gap. Sergeant Dudley mouthed something rude, cut his engine and got out, putting on his uniform cap to denote he was in business.

'What is it *now*? This bloody village ...'

'Big Alsatian ... frightening the cows ...'

'Well, thank God. I thought perhaps your sewage-farm was blowing up again. Stray dogs we can cope with ... where is it?'

They looked, they climbed through the hedge and peered both ways. No sign.

'It was a big black thing, with a collar and medal ...'

'You didn't get a chance to look at the medal ...?'

'No – but it was a sort of star-shape.'

'I'll put in a report and keep my eyes open ... Sewage-works OK? *Quite sure*? Right then ...' He got back in his car and drove away. As the back of the Panda vanished round the bend, Ralph could not but look back at the gap in the hedge ...

But nothing showed. And then, with a sudden rush that joggled his unsettled nerves, the collies were back, same as ever, all fear forgotten.

Encouraged, he tried the cows again.

They trundled past the gap without a qualm.

He got them into their stalls, made sure they had forage and water, and started milking. Jack Norton, his back apparently quite recovered, but still smelling strongly of beer, came in to complain that Ralph was running late . . .

Ralph sighed and kept at it, after Jack had gone, drawing comfort from the massive warmth of the cows, their enormous, milky maternity, the sweet, grassy smell of their breath. Cows always soothed him; he almost dozed on his feet. That *damned* dog . . . he thought sleepily . . . making me all late . . . late for tea and Mam will play hell. He tried to remember exactly what the dog had looked like, in case the police wanted a complete description . . .

And then he remembered what had been most queer about it. And even amid all that bovine warmth, his skin crept.

It had not had its paws on the top rail of the fence.

It had been *gripping* the top rail, as a man might stand and grip it. But no dog could grip a fence that way; dogs didn't have fingers. This dog had fingers. Long, black, hairy fingers.

Prepoc had had fingers.

This dog had stood upright.

Prepoc had stood upright.

And he somehow sensed the dog was evil . . .

Jack Norton came back, and said since the milking was nearly finished, would Ralph take the cows back up the field?

'I'm sorry, Mr Norton I feel sick. Can you do it? I'll finish up here, and see to the cooler . . .'

Jack looked at him closely, under the neon lights of the milking-parlour.

'You do look a bit off, lad. Reet pale an' sweaty. What's tha been eating? Run along home – I'll finish up here.'

Ralph ran all the way, feeling a total coward. Why didn't he warn Mr Norton about the dog-thing?

Maybe the dog-thing didn't want Mr Norton . . .

But he waited by his bedroom window that evening, until he saw Jack Norton drive safely past, on his way down to the pub at Melmerby.

CHAPTER 6

'I'm just slipping next door,' said Mam. 'He's been bashing her again, poor soul, an' she's a bit low. By God,' she added savagely, 'I'd soon settle his hash if he was mine. Off to the pub three nights a week on his wages, an' what's the end of it, he comes home an' gives her a right shiner. And in front of young Ruby too. If he don't lay off her soon, I'll go an' sort him whether he's mine or not.'

Ralph, watching his mother putting on her old blue working anorak and stooping to the spotted mirror of the Victorian sideboard to run a comb carelessly through her brown hair, could not but feel a tremor for thin, weedy Bert Todd next door, with his wrinkled drinker's forehead and sweaty pallor that made him look as if he'd just got out of bed, no matter what time of day it was. If Mam once started she'd make mincemeat of him. Mam was six feet tall. Ever since he could remember, Mam had been like a warrior queen. When they'd read about Boadicea at school, rousing the Iceni and massacring the Roman legions, it had been Mam he'd seen in Boadicea's chariot. She looked a bit like Britannia; even a bit like Margaret Thatcher, except she never went to the hairdresser's for back-combing, because she hadn't money to waste on that rubbish.

He'd always been a bit scared of her; still was. But she made him feel very safe. His school life had been littered with the remains of his enemies, boys *and* teachers. It wasn't that he told tales to Mam; she just somehow *knew* when someone was making him unhappy; then that someone copped it. Funny, the Head could go on bleating at Fatty Higginson for years, trying to stop his bullying. To no effect. Mam had put her hand across Higginson's face *once* and Higginson . . . well . . . never touched Ralph again. Or any of Higginson's friends, either. Ralph had spent half his schooldays pleading with Mam not to deal with people; it was so profoundly embarrassing.

She gave him a sharp look now. 'You didn't eat much tea – no seconds at all. You ailing for something?'

'No Mam!' He couldn't help his voice rising to a desperate squeak.

'Old Jack Norton been putting on you?'

'No, Mam.'

'Something's bothering you,' she said darkly. 'You may hide it from some. You won't hide it from me.'

'No, Mam.'

She waited, watching him with all the force of her blue eyes. He felt his walls crumbling inside. If she'd stared at him a bit longer, he'd have given in, and babbled all about the creature in the field. But just before he opened his mouth, she gave a snort and returned her attention to the evils of 'im next door.

'He'd better be out, or leaving her be. That's all I can say.' She went, with a pot of her damson jam in one hand; she never went anywhere without a little present in her hand.

He heard the latch click shut. The silence descended, and he began to think about the creature in the field. It was almost as if the creature took over his mind, the moment Mam let go of it. He got up and unsnibbed the lock on the back door; it shot home with a reassuring click. Then he went round the house, checking all the window-fastenings, upstairs as well. Then he got Dad's old shotgun, loaded it with Togger's cartridges, but didn't put on the safety-catch, and laid it on the bare wood table. The gun had never left his side in the week since he had seen the creature; he carried it wherever he went. It had got to be a village joke. Because, although he always said it was for shooting rabbits, he could never actually bring himself to shoot any . . .

He tried to settle to his *Guinness Book of Records*, but found himself reading about the tallest man in the world over and over again. He wondered sadly if he was going mad, like old Mr Leese at Holly Cottage, who every spring greeted the little green men who appeared in his garden . . .

The creature, the dog-thing, had been hanging around the whole week. Never so close again; but sometimes when Ralph looked up suddenly from his work, he would see a dark shape behind a thin, dying hedge; or seemed to see a pair of dark, pricked ears, just sinking out of sight behind a stone wall.

He'd managed to set up one defence against it. He'd spread the word that it really was a savage Alsatian that had attacked the cows. The village men had believed *that* fast enough; there'd been plenty of killer-dogs in the past, and dogs shot before they'd even been proved guilty. Togger had spotted it, and Jack Norton; and old

41

Jeff Lawson, the keeper at Unthank Hall, had managed a long-distance shot, to no effect. That proved to Ralph he wasn't totally deluded. And it had seemed to keep the thing at bay.

At least by day. But now Ralph found himself listening, listening. It was getting a little dark; only a cloudy evening in July at nine o'clock. But a little dark . . . he went across and switched the light on. Then realized the lit room would show him up to anything lurking outside, and drew the curtains. Then wished he hadn't drawn the curtains, because he couldn't see outside. So he drew the curtains back again, and put off the light and sat in the dark. Staring at the window, expecting any moment the prick-eared head to rise above the sill and the pot of geraniums that Mam kept there.

Then he felt that funny feeling he'd felt so many times recently; of the air falling apart; of the air going hollow. And he knew the creature was near again.

But he was still shocked, when its head rose up outside the window, behind the geraniums. He'd never believed it would dare come this near Mam's domain. This wasn't the schoolyard, where anything could happen; or some back-alley on the way home from school . . . This was *home*.

And the realization so terrified him that he was quite unable to move. He could only look at the loaded gun, lying useless on the table in front of him.

The creature put one paw on the windowsill outside, then the other. It was almost as if it wanted him to see its long black, hairy fingers.

And then, as if in the worst of a nightmare, the hands touched the window, and the window-handles began to turn, inside, of their own accord. And then the two halves of the window began to separate, move outwards. As they opened full, the curtains, caught by a little cool evening breeze, billowed inwards into the room.

The creature looked at Ralph; its eyes, like any dog's, were almost human. But they didn't offer worship, beg for love, like a normal dog's eyes. These eyes pried, understood, *commanded*.

And Ralph knew now it was not a real dog. Its shoulders were too broad; its chest, under the long, black hair, was muscled like a man's; its legs were too thick; it had always walked upright . . . he remembered stories of werewolves, lining a churchyard wall, scrabbling in graves . . .

The creature raised one long-fingered paw, and beckoned to Ralph, quite slowly and gently. And as in a nightmare, he found himself rising to his feet, taking one tiny step forward. He knew he would go with the creature . . . he looked at its open mouth, the lolling tongue, the big canine teeth, stained brown at the roots, just like Jet's and Nance's.

Another step . . .

Then the door-handle rattled behind Ralph. The door was thumped, angrily. The creature's eyes wavered for a moment, uncertain. Then the sound of a key in the lock. And still the creature hovered, wavered.

The door opened, and shut. 'What the heck you got the door locked for, Ralph? Scared o' burglars or summat? At your age – a big lad like you? Mrs Todd gave me some delphiniums – she's a well-meaning soul, but they're half-dead, poor things.' Mam bustled in, her big red hands already plucking condemned delphiniums from the rest of the bunch, ready to throw in the waste-bin. Her head was down. She never even saw the creature. 'What you standing there for, Ralph, like one o'clock half-struck? Fetch me the blue vase from under the sink . . . Go on, what's the matter with you?'

Then she looked up, following the direction of Ralph's gaze, and saw the creature.

She screamed; though whether from terror or rage or both, Ralph could never afterwards tell. But her big hands reached instinctively on to the table for something to throw. And found the loaded shotgun . . . She hadn't been a farmer's wife for nothing. She'd lived for forty years with dogs mauling sheep and foxes killing chickens.   --

At the last second, Ralph saw the creature's eyes change, flare with alarm; and realized it was no invincible spook.

Then both barrels of the shotgun went off ear-splitting, one just after the other, and the room was filled with the sharp, Guy-Fawkes smell of cordite. Ralph, half-blinded, heard a heavy body thump down hard outside the window. When he looked again, the window was empty.

'Nasty great thing,' spat Mam. 'What did you have the window open for, Ralph? Just look at them curtains . . . ruined. Go and see if it's dead. Put it out of its misery.' She handed him the gun. Her hands weren't even shaking. But his were, as he reloaded, and then crept round the corner of the house.

It was lying there, a huge black shape in the gathering dusk, quite still.

'Put the kitchen light on, Mam,' he called, quaveringly.

The light came on, but it didn't help much. Mam only used forty-watt bulbs . . . He was glad, really. He didn't really want to see it. He knew what a shotgun at close range could do. But he could tell from the flat way it was sprawled that it was dead. No sound of its breathing.

'It's dead, Mam.'

She looked out of the window. 'By gum, it's a whopper. Dogs that size shouldn't be allowed. You'd better go an' ring the poliss. Musta belonged to somebody. 'Less it came out of a circus.' Then she closed the window with a double thud, and drew the tattered remnants of the curtains, swoosh, swoosh, already wondering loudly whether she had another pair that would fit.

He ran to the phone box at the far end of the village, dialled 999, told them, and ran back home. He'd have another look at the thing in the garden, once the police had come with their torches . . .

Mam plonked a mug of tea in front of him. 'Sit there an' get your breath. Never seen a dog shot afore? You *have* led a sheltered life . . . I hope it didn't belong to nobody important – I've got no money to give them. They had no call to let it stray.'

Sergeant Dudley finished his pint-pot of tea, and dried his neat, ginger moustache with a spotless white handkerchief. He put his uniform cap back on.

'Let's have a look at the thing, then. I don't want it mucking up the boot of my car.' He picked up his large black polythene sack, a bit like a bin-liner, with some distaste. Ralph, looking at the size of the sack, thought sickly that the sergeant was due for a shock . . .

They trooped round the corner. 'We haven't had any Alsatian strays reported,' said the sergeant, 'so I doubt we'll get a complaint. I just don't want it mucking up the boot of my car.'

He shone his torch below the window.

There was nothing there.

'Where did you report the body was lying?' A hardness had come into the sergeant's voice; he was remembering this was Pottyville.

'It was there,' said Ralph. 'It was dead.'

'I know what I shot,' said Mam, ominously.

'Well,' said the sergeant, wisely pouring oil on troubled water, 'there's bloodstains . . . *and* up the path here . . . and in the road. You can see where it's dragged itself.'

His big torch flickered authoritatively, here and there, like an usherette's in a cinema. 'It won't get far – lost too much blood. I think we better wait to report it, till we've found the body. Hallo, what's this?'

He picked up something that lay glinting on the path. A star of metal, much battered by lead shot. It glinted yellowly in the light of the torch.

'It was wearing that on a collar round its neck,' said Ralph.

'That's evidence, then,' said the sergeant. He slipped it in his pocket. 'Mebbe we can use it to trace the owner. Good-nights apiece.'

And he drove away.

'But it was *dead*,' said Ralph.

'Very strong, animals are,' said Mam. 'And they'll always crawl away to die in secret, if they can. Come in before you catch your death of cold. I've never seen a lad for shivering like you.'

CHAPTER 7

There came a timid tapping on the kitchen door. It made Ralph jump, even after three days.

'Come in,' shouted Mam. 'It's not locked!'

There was a vague bumping against the door, then Mrs Norton was standing there, a huge, dribbly, black polythene bucket in either hand. 'I wonder,' she said apologetically, 'if Ralph would mind feeding the hens in the top field and locking them up for the night? Jack's back's bad again . . .'

Ralph closed his eyes, cursed Jack's drunken idleness, and thought it was the end of the world. The top field was half a mile from the village; even beyond the cows' field. And twice already today the air had started falling apart, and he'd fled from his work, back towards the safety of the village.

There were two more dog-things, see. When he'd looked in the garden, the morning after the shooting, he'd seen quite clearly where the creature's body had been dragged away. There were black hairs, stuck to the top of the fence with blood. And close by, two huge sets of deep pad-prints in the loose soil, where they'd lifted the dead one over . . .

Two of them. Oh, they'd grown very cautious; they'd learnt about shotguns. And they didn't want anyone to know they were there either; that's why they must've come back for the dead one. Within view of the village, Ralph knew he was safe. But the hens' field was clean over the hill.

'Go on, then!' said Mam. 'Get on wi' it, Ralph. That'll be an hour's overtime for Ralph, Mrs Norton, by the time he's got there an' back.'

Mrs Norton sighed, at the price of her husband's idleness.

'I don't feel well, Mam,' said Ralph stubbornly. 'I've got that gut-ache again.'

'I'll go if you like, Mrs Norton,' said Ruby Todd, rising from the fireplace corner. 'I was just going home anyway.'

Ruby was the only female under twenty tolerated in Mam's house.

46

Twice, Ralph had tried bringing girlfriends home for tea. The spread Mam had laid on had been splendiferous. But then Mam had started saying all the wrong things; got out the family photograph album, with toddler Ralph stark naked, paddling in a muddy rock-pool at Blackpool. Mam had talked heavily of poverty, of Ralph being her sole support, of the price of setting up a home and the agonies of childbearing, till Ralph had wearied of blushing. Neither girl had wanted to know him after that.

But Ruby was tolerated; she lived next door. Ruby had toddled round Mam's kitchen since she was knee-high; become part of the furniture. On the other hand, Ruby had changed a lot in the last two years. Her slightly dirty bare legs had become graceful and slender; her faded pink sweater had filled out becomingly. Her hair hung long, dark and straight below her shoulders, even though it could always do with a wash. And though her nose was a bit beaky, she had lovely eyes. Ralph wondered if Mam never noticed that Ruby was becoming a woman. Ralph dreamt of a Ruby bathed and spotless, clad in nylon tights and new clothes, with her hair washed till it shone like silk. She was nice to talk to, sympathetic. And best of all, she seemed not to have noticed she'd become a woman ... no embarrassing make-up, or giving herself airs or giggling. Ralph often wondered how Ruby would react if he tried to kiss her; he would, one day.

But then sometimes he wondered if that was exactly what Mam wanted; whether Mam had already chosen Ruby ready-made, to marry him and move into this cottage, so life could go on exactly as before ... and that was enough to spoil any day-dream completely.

And here was Ruby standing up, her shapely legs nearly hidden inside old wellies, and saying she would go to the top field to feed the hens. Suppose the creatures took Ruby instead, and she vanished into the dusk, never to be seen again?

It was not to be borne; he got up heavily, picked up the shotgun from the corner, and shoved the two remaining shells in his pocket.

'I'll come with you, Ruby,' he said. 'Easier for two.'

'What you want that stupid old gun for?' asked Mam. 'Put it back where it belongs to be.'

'Rabbits,' he snapped, abruptly.

'You'll never get a rabbit wi' the grass this wet!'

'Best time. C'mon, Ruby.'

As they passed the farm, the dogs came out of their kennel,

stretching and waving their tails. It had been raining all day; they'd been idle and were keen for a run.

'C'mon, Jet! C'mon, Nance!' Why not? Safety in numbers. And the dogs were his eyes and ears . . .

It was a strange evening. It had stopped raining, and there was sun, somewhere above the murk. But they walked through a heat-mist like golden smoke, that loaded every leaf with moisture and turned the distant trees to faint ghosts. Ruby carried one bucket; they carried another between them, and Ralph carried the gun in his right hand. Ruby was unashamedly delighted to be out with him; she was really lit up, exclaiming over everything she saw: spiderwebs in the hedges, festooned with jewels of moisture; a blue butterfly on a stem of couch-grass, fluttering its wings to dry them. It made Ruby seem fragile and precious, in a way she never had before; because always in the back of his mind he saw again the creature standing upright, behind the gap in the hedge, its long, black fingers clutching the top rail of the fence . . . They would not get her; he would kill them first.

As they approached the gap in the hedge, he stopped and put down the bucket and loaded the gun.

'What you doin' that for, Ralph? Ain't no old rabbits round here. That's dangerous . . .'

'Never you mind.' He picked up the bucket and began walking again. The gap came in sight.

'Stop fiddling wi' them triggers, Ralph. You're making me nervous. Who d'you think you are – Billy the Kid? Oh, you do look gloomy. Don't you like company?'

'Let's get past this gap in the hedge.'

But they passed the gap without incident. The dogs were happy enough, scouring the hedgerows, cocking their legs, their thin plumes of tails waving gaily. But all he could think of was the endless bends of the mist-shrouded road they were leaving behind them. And the fact that he was leading Ruby deeper and deeper into danger, which she didn't deserve. It was him the creatures wanted, not her. Him because of Prepoc. He should send her back. But he was desperately afraid of being alone. And with her there as a witness, they might still leave him be. They didn't like being noticed. But he had no right to hide behind Ruby like a coward . . .

His dilemma became unbearable, and came out in a strangled yelp.

'Go home, Ruby. Now!' He shouted at her like she was Jet or Nance.

48

She glared at him, hurt and angry. 'Don't you start giving me orders. I'm not your servant, Ralph Edwards. If you don't want my company, you've only got to say . . .' Tears appeared in the corners of her eyes. She looked so forlorn that Ralph's heart nearly broke.

'It's not that – it's going to rain soon, Ruby – rain really hard.'

She softened immediately. Put a work-callused hand on his arm. 'I don't mind a bit of old rain, Ralph. Bit o' rain never hurt nobody.' She picked up her bucket again, saying, as if that settled the matter, 'You can't carry two buckets *and* a gun.'

He gave in, after a last, checking glance at the still-happy dogs.

They reached the hen-huts, and poured the food into the filthy troughs, half an inch deep in stuck-on feed. The white hens came scurrying from all over the field, and settled in a pecking, feathery mass around their legs.

Beyond, the vale stretched away in a ghostly light, belt after belt of trees, till it vanished into the mist.

'Creepy, innit?' said Ruby. She was hugging herself with shapely bare arms that had gone goose-pimpled and purple, rather unbecomingly. 'I think you're right about that storm coming. My head feels sort of ringy, all of a sudden . . .'

Ralph swore horribly, shockingly, into the silence that was gathering beyond the tapping of the hens' beaks on the wooden troughs. The air *was* starting to fall apart, and he knew himself for a fool.

Of course the creatures hadn't shown themselves before, near the village. If they had, he'd have tipped the hen-feed into the ditch and run for it.

But now they were coming for him; even though he had somebody else with him. And they didn't like leaving witnesses . . .

If they came and Ruby saw them, they'd take her as well. He knew it with sickening certainty.

She put her hand to her head, spreading her fingers over her eyes. 'I keep getting these funny feelings in my head – like a headache starting, only it never comes to nothing. Everybody keeps getting them – d'you think there's a bug going about, Ralph?'

When he didn't answer, she dropped her hand and looked at him. 'What's the matter, Ralph, you look scared to death?' She followed the direction of his eyes. 'Ralph, what's up wi' dogs? What's up wi' hens?'

The dogs had backed, snarling, into the sheltered corner between the two hen-huts. The hens were wandering round in confused circles, their food forgotten.

'Ralph, what's going on? I feel my head's going to burst . . .'

'Get behind me!' He swept his left arm round to push her into the corner with the dogs.

'What you doin' – that *hurt*!'

'Get *behind* me!' He backed into her, driving her deeper into the corner to safety. If there was any safety. He stood, a dog cringing and growling against each leg, the hens clustering up in front of him, as he swung the barrels of the shotgun from side to side, covering the whole field. While Ruby kept demanding, 'What's the matter, Ralph? What's the MATTER?'

He thought he could see them now, moving behind the hedge; gaps in the hedge kept darkening, then going light again. Was that the prick of dark ears, by that oak tree? Sickly, he sensed there were more than two of them. And he only had two shells for the gun . . . useless. Yet still he swung the barrels from side to side automatically, while, to his panic-stricken eyes, black shapes seemed to flicker everywhere. Were there *more* creeping up behind the hen-huts?

'Ralph, *look*! What *are* they?' Ruby's voice wasn't so much terrified as awestruck. And she wasn't pointing at the hedge, she was pointing at the sky.

They came floating down the ghastly light of the vale. Three huge shapes like hovering aircraft, solidifying through the mist.

'What are they Ralph – Hawker Harriers?'

'Yeah – expect so,' said Ralph, to keep her calm. But they were no more Harriers than he was. Unless the mature trees they were passing over were no more than tiny bushes. These things were gigantic, unearthly. They were matt black, seeming to absorb the light, and totally *silent*. Like creatures stalking their prey, their sharp down-turned noses turned a little this way, a little that.

'Ralph – how can they fly with no noise?'

'Oh, it's amazing what they can do these days.' But his voice was cracked, from a dry throat.

The middle craft, very close and huge now, nosed at them, then nosed away to the left. At them again, and away to the left again.

Ralph thought, with a pitiful rush of gladness, it doesn't want *us*, it doesn't want *us*.

Then there was a slight bang, and there was a curtain of tiny silvery particles, falling just in front of his nose.

'Ralph, that's not rain, is it?' Ruby's voice had risen to a squeal. Ralph poked at the curtain with the barrel of his gun. The gun bonked against it; it was hard and immovable like steel.

'Must be a force-field,' he muttered to himself.

'You mean – like they have on "Star Trek"?'

'Yeah,' he said reassuringly. 'Like on "Star Trek".'

'I didn't know they had them in real life . . .'

'There's a lot the government don't tell *us*!' He glanced about; the glittering force-field lay all round them, encircling the dogs and hens and the hen-huts themselves. Ralph felt trapped, like those poor bees he'd caught in flower-filled jam jars as a kid. Just as helpless as the frantically buzzing bees, just as baffled.

Then there was a much bigger bang. The force-field shook as if hit by a mighty fist; its particles danced in mad circles . . . another huge bang, and again the force-field was shaken.

Someone had trapped them, and someone else was trying to smash them out of the trap. They were being fought over, by huge forces they could never understand. Like poor, frantic, uncomprehending bees . . . All he could do was press Ruby deeper into her corner. She had her arms around him tight, now. Seeking comfort, but somehow giving it as well. It helped. As did the dogs shaking and panting against his legs.

There was an instant stab of light from the leading ship; instantly gone. Then a great gnarled oak across the field, and a whole length of hedge with it, was no longer there. Clipped off vertically at both ends, like a yard of cloth.

Another stab of light, *from* the hedge this time, upwards, towards the leading craft. As it hit, the craft seemed to break into four pieces; but when he looked again, it had become four separate craft, each spinning at immense speed into a different part of the sky. Unbelievable. He knew he was gaping like a yokel.

Again the stabbing light upwards from the hedge; he hardly heard the bangs any more; his ears were going numb. One of the spinning craft seemed to explode; but it just vanished, leaving no trace of wreckage; and the other three spinning craft danced on.

Then the whole sky darkened. All the ships vanished. Because the sky was no longer sky, but a huge, steely mirror that reflected the earth below. What Ralph saw above him was no longer clouds, but

51

upside-down reflections of trees and hedges, spread all across the sky like an upside-down map.

Then another stab of light from the mirror-sky, and another section of hedge was cut away; and another, and another. Ralph became afraid there'd be nothing left.

Then, away on the right, he saw another craft rising above the remains of the hedge. Not black this time, but shining silver like a mirror. Then it seemed to spread and spread sideways, like an egg cracked in a frying-pan. Longer and longer it grew; then split into ten separate mirror-craft.

Then the great mirror in the sky vanished, and the clouds were back, and they were full of craft twisting and turning, vanishing and reappearing without warning, till Ralph's brain spun so much he felt it must be running out of his ears. The sudden beams of light became a continuous flicker, and the bangs a rolling thunder that brattled in echoes off the distant fellside.

And still he held the shotgun aimed pointlessly in front of him. Ruby was coiled against him like a second skin, her arms so tight he could hardly breathe. And the dogs just a silent quiver against his ankles. And he knew the craft were fighting to a death he'd never understand, and that he and Ruby were the prize. And the ones that won would come for them. And he wanted the black ones to win; for no reason he could understand, because there were more of them and it seemed unfair.

Then suddenly, it was all over. There were only four craft left, all perfectly still, and the mirror-ship was in the middle. From the black ships, thin beams of still, white light centred on the mirror-ship, making it seem like a fly caught in a spider's web.

Below, the familiar green earth had been cut into a chequer-board of destruction. Like an overused target late at night in a fairground shooting-gallery. Ralph could have wept for the lost oaks; but instead his belly crept, knowing that the black craft would come for him.

And yet, for some reason, he was not quite as afraid as he should have been.

One black ship came down very close. It had no windows; it might have been an empty machine. But Ralph suddenly knew why he'd wanted the black ships to win. Their shapes were vaguely familiar; not the same but similar ... and on their sides, the same golden sunburst that had hung round Prepoc's neck.

52

They were Prepoc's people.

He gave a glad, incoherent sob, and ran out to meet them.

But the force-field still held him back.

Then the craft turned its nose away; not interested.

There was another bang, and the first bit of hedge with its oak tree was restored. Then the second, then the third. Slowly the landscape he knew was fitted back together like a jigsaw-puzzle.

'Oh, Ralph, what are they doing? What are they DOING?'

He turned to comfort her. When he looked back, the craft had gone; and the force-field. The thrushes were singing again, in the darkening hedgerows. He felt the dogs relax; stretch, shake their heads till their ears rattled. And the white hens they'd come to feed so long ago began to sort themselves out from the mountain of feathers they'd made, and peck with interest at the hen-feed still lying in the troughs. All but two, which lay still warm, but quiet and dead, suffocated in the midst of that white feathery mountain. Ralph picked them up and swung them sadly and uselessly by the legs.

Prepoc's people had gone; Prepoc's people did not want him.

'Ralph, what was it – flying saucers?' Ruby's eyes were like saucers themselves.

It was kindest to say yes. She looked very pale and ill, but oddly triumphant.

'Cor, we'll be famous now. Let's ring up the papers. I've got plenty of 10p pieces.' She scrabbled her purse out of her skirt-pocket with trembling eager fingers. Her face looked like Christmas Day.

'Depends who else saw them,' he said heavily. 'We're behind the hill . . . look at the mist . . . who's going to believe *us*? Who's going to believe anybody from Pottyville?'

'What else could they say it *was*?'

'A thunderstorm – sheet-lightning – ball-lightning.'

'If only you'd had your camera . . .'

'They'd only say we faked the pictures . . .'

'Oh, *Ralph!*' Her face fell, and his heart moved for her.

And just at that moment, from the heavy clouds above, the first bolt of genuine blue lightning fell. And the rain came down in solid rods, washing away the last of her hopes, and turning her faded pink T-shirt transparent in the most disturbing way. He hugged her, as the white hens scurried past to the shelter of the huts. When they were all inside he dropped the door-hatches and wearily picked up the empty black buckets.

'Oh, Ralph, won't no one believe us?'

'They wouldn't believe Jack Norton about the sewage-farm, love. They wouldn't believe a whole village.'

'Oh, you've never called me "love" before. Give us another hug.' She snuggled into him, like a half-drowned kitten, as they slowly made their way back to the road.

There was a cheerful double-honk; then a Post Office van was pulling up, lights glistening through the downpour, windscreen-wipers working nineteen to the dozen. The side-window was wound down rapidly, and Postie's bald head thrust out.

'Hop in, kids, before you catch your death. What weather to pick for canoodling!'

'We've been feeding the hens,' said Ralph stiffly, pushing Ruby into the van in front of him.

'Never heard it called that before,' said Postie, with a heavy knowing wink. 'She'll have to sit on your knee, Ralph. Don't expect that'll be any hardship. Quite a little storm, isn't it, Ruby? Never seen such lightning. Still, it's an ill-wind isn't it, Ruby?' He grinned at her in mock-lechery. Nobody minded Postie's cracks; which was just as well, as he never stopped making them. 'Mind where you put them buckets, Ralph. We don't want hen-grit all over the Royal Mail, do we?'

They swept on towards the village. 'Never known such a storm,' went on Postie. 'Haven't seen a soul stirring out of doors this side of Langwathby. Lots o' cars pulled in by the roadside – water in their electrics, I suppose. Bet there'll be chaos on the M6 . . .'

Grimly, Ralph wondered if Prepoc's people could control the weather too. Certainly it had kept their battle wonderfully private.

CHAPTER 8

They lay snugged up on the lower fell; in a round space trampled out of the shoulder-high bracken, where only the flies came to bother them.

Far off, the mountains of Lakeland dreamed misty as ghosts; sure sign of fine weather. Below, where they'd parked the scrambler, an endless line of Sunday buses and cars climbed Hartside Height, the noise of their engines as distantly romantic as waves breaking on a beach.

Ralph felt infinitely peaceful. A week without a trace of the dog-things. The world was clean. Prepoc's people had *extracted* them like an agonizing tooth.

Ruby wriggled even closer; rearranged his arm to suit her comfort, selected a succulent piece of grass and bit into it.

'Nice.'

Ralph took his eyes from the high, blue heavens, and kissed the face she proffered, with rather abstract enjoyment. They'd been lying kissing two hours, and he felt full of it, like after Sunday dinner. Who wanted to eat again, straight after Sunday dinner? He wanted to lie and think about Prepoc.

Still, he was pretty pleased with Ruby. She'd taken to washing her hair every night, and it shone like black silk. And she'd bought this smashing ethnic skirt at Penrith Oxfam for four quid. And she smelt of eau-de-Cologne, though not enough to choke you, like some. If only she'd wear tights, he'd be proud to take her to meet the Queen . . .

What was more, she'd made it quite clear that *she* wasn't going to live with any ma-in-law when *she* got married. And she had nearly a thousand pounds saved up from her job on the check-out at Penrith. Ralph, who only had the five hundred pounds that Dad had left him, plus interest, was tremendously impressed.

'Give us another kiss . . . or are you dreaming about your other woman? Johnny Sligo used to do that – that's why I dumped him.

You're nicer than him. You talk to a girl like she's a human being, even while you're doing it . . .'

'Doing *what?*' yelped Ralph. 'I haven't done nothing much . . .'

'So you'd tell Vicar what you *have* been doing to me?'

'Shurrup!' He wriggled uncomfortably. She giggled, and kissed right inside his ear with a hot tongue. He didn't like that much; it left a cold, wet feeling afterwards. He waited till she'd turned away, and wiggled his ear dry with a finger of his free hand.

'Don't you like having your ear kissed?' she asked, without opening her eyes.

'You're so sharp you'll cut yourself.'

'I wonder who they were,' she said in a dreaming voice.

'Who?' he asked grumpily, though he knew damn well who.

'The little green men in their flying saucers . . .'

He was sick to death of her little-green-man routine, especially in that dreamy, wondering voice. A prick of self-importance tempted him. 'They weren't little green men.' The moment he said it, he knew he shouldn't have.

She shot upright and stared at him, thrusting long white fingers, less rough than they used to be, through her long dark hair. Pushing it up on top of her head, exposing her long, white, kissable neck like Marie Antoinette going to the guillotine . . .

'How do you know?' she asked, eyes sharp.

'You know that Alsatian me Mam shot . . . well that was one of them. Only they walk on their hind legs and they've got fingers . . .'

She screamed; with that enjoyment he could never understand in girls. 'Go on, pull the other leg, it's got bells on it . . . what a horrible mind you got, Ralph Edwards. I mean, fancy it coming up behind you and putting its horrible long hairy fingers on . . .' Her pupils went huge with some internal festival of horror. 'They wouldn't let them,' she finished, doubtfully.

'Well, if it was only an Alsatian, where *is* it? Sergeant Dudley said it'd lost too much blood to get far. A thing that size – we'd be smelling it by now.'

'It crawled into some hole to die.'

'A thing that size'd need a railway tunnel. It was *huge* . . .' Some devil was driving him on, against all sense.

'Oh, Ralph, *stop* it. Or I won't go with you any more. Give us another kiss, I've turned cold all over – *feel!*'

After ten minutes, she sat up again. 'You were kidding, weren't you? I gotta sleep tonight.'

'Yeah, I was kidding,' he said, glad to be off the hook.

But with Ruby, getting off the hook wasn't all that easy. Easier to put something in her mind than get it out again.

'You were awfully scared that day. You pretended you had gut-ache, so you wouldn't have to go and feed the hens. And you kept playing with that loaded shotgun. Ralph, you were terrified before anything *happened*!'

'I was only thinking of kissing you ... and terrified you mightn't ...'

But he was always a rotten liar. She pulled away and huddled and stared at him with accusing eyes.

'That's the first time you ever lied to me, Ralph Edwards. I don't want to go with somebody who tells me lies – got plenty of those from Johnny Sligo.'

And with a sinking heart he knew she meant it. If he did tell her another lie, she would know and pack him in. She added in a low voice, 'When that battle was all over – you shouted something to that black plane. Like you knew somebody inside – like you were glad they'd come. Tell me the truth, Ralph!'

He was silent; it was impossible. He wanted to be faithful to Ruby; but he wanted to be faithful to Prepoc as well. There was no answer.

She got up, making a great show of it, dusting herself down, picking up her handbag. 'Don't bother – I'll walk home by meself. Goodbye, Ralph.'

He let her get twenty yards, then he couldn't bear it any more.

'Ruby – come back – I'll tell you.'

She came back with such alacrity that, just for a moment, he hated her. She'd forced him. So he didn't mince it. He told her everything he knew about the dog-things.

'Oh, Ralph, it's *true*! I can't *bear* it! What'll they do next?' She stood up and looked wildly in all directions, over the tops of the bracken.

He took her hand gently, still sitting down. 'It's all right, love. Prepoc's lot came and took them away. I think they're sort of ... policemen.'

'Who's *Prepoc*?' If anything, she looked more alarmed than ever.

'He's a sort of ... cat. Only he's big too, and walks on his hind legs, and he's got fingers as well ...'

'And I suppose he's appearing in *Puss in Boots* at Penrith Civic Hall next Christmas? D'you think I'm totally stupid, Ralph Edwards?

Ooh, I could *kill* you – you nearly had me believing in them dogs . . . Ooooh!' She pushed him flat, hammering her slender fists into his recumbent stomach, and he couldn't even retaliate for giggling. 'I'll teach you to tell me lies . . . lying there laughing . . .'

Then, abruptly, in that way he hadn't learnt to cope with, she stopped hitting him and stared off down the hillside, back stiff with disapproval. She might be moody for hours now, ruining the whole day. But she'd given him another chance to keep Prepoc safe. Oh, heck, she'd get over it; they always did.

Then he saw the drop of water hit her skirt; and another, and another. He looked up, thinking it was starting to rain. But the sky was still peerless blue.

She was crying. And even more terrifying, she was crying silently. On the few occasions Mam had ever cried, she cried silently. So Ralph felt silent crying was close to the end of the world. He didn't dare touch Ruby; she might explode. But he couldn't just go on sitting there. It became more and more unbearable. So he finally said:

'I'll show you if you like.'

'Show me what?' Her voice was muffled, and the drops still kept hitting her skirt.

'Where Prepoc's buried. It's a grave – he's dead.'

She swung round with a red-eyed glare. 'If you think you're getting me down one of your stupid old lead-mines in me best Sunday clothes . . .'

'It's not down a lead-mine – he's in the open. But I'll show you – if you promise not to breathe a word to a soul – *ever*!'

It was her turn to quail, before his ferocity. 'I promise. Where is it?'

'Up there – inside that cairn.'

'Walk all the way up there – in this heat? This better *not* be a joke, Ralph Edwards.'

She had to take off her high heels, and slither barefoot over the tussocks, which she said prickled her feet. They sweated. She lagged behind, complaining. He had to keep on stopping to wait for her. In the end he got fed up, and walked on ahead where he couldn't hear her endless stream of complaints. It wasn't a happy outing.

It didn't feel like something that could change the fate of the universe, either.

*

They knelt amidst the tumbled stones, and stared at the face of Prepoc.

'He should be in a museum,' breathed Ruby, awed. 'Ralph, you're *famous*! Like that little girl that discovered them dinosaur bones . . .'

'How would you like to be stuffed an' put in a museum when you were dead, with everybody staring at you?'

'I would if I died young an' beautiful,' said Ruby wistfully. 'Fellers would come an' fall in love with me, a thousand years in the future . . .' Then, practically, 'What's in them Easter-egg things?'

He took out the red-lustre egg, and offered a dab of its contents to her mouth.

'What does that make you do?' she asked suspiciously. 'Is it an aphro . . . aphro . . . does it make you come all over sexy?'

'No . . . promise.' She licked; she stood tall; her eyes shone. She looked like some great queen out of *Lord of the Rings*, shaped before the seas were born . . .

Finally she sat down and said, 'People would pay money to feel like that. You could sell it to ICI . . . make your fortune . . . live in a big house like Elton John.'

He looked at the peaceful face of Prepoc, and felt an utter traitor. But Ruby grabbed his arm. 'Think what you could do for other people, Ralph. You could buy your Mam one of them new bungalows and she'd never have to go cleaning for that old bitch at Unthank Hall again . . . Ralph, be *practical*!'

He looked up at her, exasperated. Couldn't she understand what that would mean? Then he said, 'I don't want him mucked about. If them scientists knew he was here, they'd cut him up to find out how he worked. Then display him as a freakshow.'

'Not if you only took a couple of them eggs. You could say you just found them, miles away. Down one of your old lead-mines . . .

'*C'mon*, Ralph, d'you want to be poor all your life? D'you want me slaving at that check-out till I'm old an' grey? Ooh, my guts *do* ache, and all the old cows are tryin' to pull a fast one over you, all the time . . .'

'All right,' he said at last. 'Two eggs and no more. No more *ever*, understand? So don't come nagging at me again. An' if it all goes wrong – if the police come an' give us the third-degree – you know *nothing*, right?'

'Yes, Ralph,' she said, ever so humbly.

He chose the black egg, which had nearly killed him; and a green-gold one he didn't know the use of.

'Why don't you take the red one?' she wheedled. 'That's the one they'll pay the money for.'

'I might need that,' he blazed.

'Why?'

'If them dog-things come back . . .' He gently fingered the blaster that lay so quiet beside Prepoc.

'But you said they weren't coming back . . .'

He replaced the blaster and clicked shut the coffin, and began piling the stones back, without another word.

Humbly, she helped him.

CHAPTER 9

Ralph was up early, Wednesday morning, and down the lane to intercept Postie, as he ground up the hill to the village in third gear. Postie pulled up, at his raised arm.

'Sorry, Ralph, nothing for your house this morning. Expecting a letter from your French mistress, are you? And don't want yer Mam to find out? Thought you was courting that Ruby Todd! Not a word, eh?' Postie put one short finger against the side of his bulbous nose, which had little ginger hairs growing out of the tip, and winked ponderously.

'No,' said Ralph. 'I gotta parcel to post. And I don't want her in the sub-post office shootin' off her mouth about it. Will you post it for me in Glassonby?'

He handed it over, with a battered pound coin on top.

Postie pushed back his cap, and scratched his bald head. 'Well, I heard o' lads your age *gettin'* parcels they didn't want their Mams to know about; specially parcels in plain, brown-paper wrappers. But I never heard o' lads *sending* parcels they didn't want their Mams to know about. By God, it's heavy for its size. What is it – the Koh-i-noor diamond? To "ICI, London", eh? "The Manager"? Ye are moving in posh circles now, Ralph . . . well, I expect it'll get there, in spite of no proper address. There's only one ICI an' I expect there's only one Manager . . .'

But in spite of all his jokes, which as usual were non-stop and always embarrassing, Postie was still waiting for an explanation . . .

Ralph had spent half the night thinking one up.

'It's my patent cure for sheep-ticks,' he said. 'An old shepherd at Melmerby Fair gave it me, an' I've tried it an' it works.'

'Well, I'm sure that'll help their export drive – specially to Australia. Probably just what they've bin waiting for, in Australia.' He pushed the parcel and pound coin into his pocket. 'Gotta help the export drive, haven't we, Maisie?' He turned and spoke to the thin scruffy mongrel that, against all Post Office regulations, often

61

accompanied him on his rounds. Maisie yapped hopefully, one paw in the air, her tin-tack claws scrabbling at the worn plastic of the front passenger-seat.

'I suppose you *have* put your name an' address inside, Ralph? We don't want you missing the rewards of your great researches . . . blushing, are yer? We still think it's a diamond tiara for your French mistress, don't we, Maisie? Bought by illegally embezzling Jack Norton's vast profits . . .'

Still chortling at his own wit, he drove off into the morning haze, his engine note altering as he changed gear. He wasn't a bad sort, for an old bachelor. He'd tried courting Mam once, sitting round her kitchen till all hours, telling his jokes and drinking endless mugs of tea. Till Mam twigged what he was up to, and sent him packing with the biggest mouthful Ralph had ever heard. But Postie still had a soft spot for Ralph.

The van vanished round the corner, like it did every morning. How was Ralph to know he'd never see it again? But he felt suddenly uneasy . . . he again checked over what they'd done.

Ruby had taken the other parcel with her to Penrith, to post on her way home at lunch-time, in the middle of the early-closing rush. Both parcels were addressed simply to 'The Manager, ICI, London', because they hadn't been able to get any address out of the telephone directory in the village phone box. Both parcels contained the same message, printed in block capitals.

'Dear Sir,
I found this egg while using my metal-detector near Long Rigg stone circle. I washed it clean – I hope that was all right. It has some strange chemical inside. Is it valuable? If so, would you like to buy it off me? If you would, please put a message in the personal column of the *Daily Telegraph*.

Yours Sincerely,
J. Henry Esq.'

They had spent a long agonizing evening in Jack Norton's hayloft, making up that letter. Ruby had pinched the wrapping-paper and string from work. She had thought of using the Personal Column of the *Daily Telegraph* which her manager brought to work every day, and left lying about once he'd read it . . .

It *seemed* foolproof . . . then a terrible thought hit Ralph. Suppose the parcels were sent on to the police? His and Ruby's fingerprints must be all over the eggs – why hadn't he thought to wipe them off?

Then he relaxed, remembering the police hadn't *got* his and Ruby's fingerprints anyway.

They were safe; Prepoc was safe; the worst that could happen was that they might scan the *Daily Telegraph* in vain . . .

And yet he stayed uneasy. What had they started? He nearly ran across to the far side of the village, to intercept Postie on his way out and get the egg back off him.

But he told himself not to be silly, and went and had his breakfast.

But he was out even earlier the following morning. He wanted to make sure Postie hadn't forgotten to post it; he wanted back the change from his pound coin, too. But above all, he wanted to be sure that everything was all *right* . . .

Postie was late this morning . . . *really* late. Ralph hovered from foot to foot, consulting his watch every minute. Reading stupidly, over and over again, the writing on the blue, plastic BOCM cattle-food sack that Bert Todd had nailed upside-down on the roof of his pigsty, in a feeble attempt to keep it waterproof. In five more minutes, he'd have to go, or he'd be late for work. Already he'd have to gulp down his breakfast . . .

Then he saw the van coming, down the little road on the far side of the valley. Being driven like the clappers! That wasn't like Postie . . .

As it approached, he waved it down in the usual way.

It very nearly didn't stop. It sounded its horn, almost ran him down, then pulled up with a screech of brakes, and a lot of angry gesticulating. The window was wound down and a strange head poked out; dark-haired, blue-jowled and furious.

'What the hell you think you're doing, kid? You nearly had me in the ditch. You a bloody lunatic or something?'

'Where's Postie?'

'You mean Arthur Doyle? You might well ask! Your friend Postie has buggered off, van an' all. And a full load of Royal Mail, *including* registereds! He's got half the police in Cumbria out looking for him. And guess who got picked to do his bloody round? These roads are a maze – I've been through Glassonby four times already . . '

'Did he *get* to Glassonby? Yesterday?'

'No, no Glassonby. Last person saw him was the postmistress here. Hope you haven't got a local highwayman, or he'll get me an' all. I'd chuck the postbags at him, the way I feel this morning.'

He drove on with a crash of gears, narrowly missing Bert Todd's sickly flock of free-range hens, and sending them squawking over the hedge in a flurry of feathers.

Cold, shaking and nearly speechless with shock, Ralph walked back to the house. The local news from Radio Carlisle was in full, crackly spate, about a suspected outbreak of swine-fever in Aspatria. Mam banged down his breakfast with more than usual force, nearly sending his plate of bacon-and-egg bouncing into his lap.

'Postie's gone missing,' said Ralph, stuffing his mouth full of bacon to stop the trembling in his voice, and jamming his knees against the table to stop them shaking. Then the bacon got stuck in his throat, and he had to throw up into his dirty handkerchief. But Mam was too busy banging about the gas stove to notice.

'I know,' Mam said, over her shoulder, 'it were on't news, poor thing. Armed robbery, they reckon. An' murder, mebbe. I don't know what this world's coming to. An' the buggers have raided the GPO at Penrith, in broad daylight – wearing fancy-dress like animals. At least in my young days they only wore nylon stockings over their heads. They didn't dress up like Rin-Tin-Tin!'

'Who's Rin-Tin-Tin?'

'A great big Alsatian, used to be on the movies, rescuing people in distress . . . seems like Rin-Tin-Tin's changed his nature. These Rin-Tin-Tins got away with six sacks of mail, yesterday. An' they cut their way through the post-office wall to do it. I'm *glad* I shot that dirty great thing that was in our garden . . . well, don't just sit there, it's gone ten past eight. D'you think Jack Norton's going to pay you for sitting on your backside doing nowt? He's a past-master at doing that for himself.'

Ralph jumped to his feet and rushed for the door in a blind panic . . .

'Don't forget your anorak – and your butties. Eeh, you'd forget your head if it was loose.'

He turned back, sandwiches in his hand, suddenly even more terrified. 'Have you seen Ruby this morning?'

'Aye – I saw her going for her bus as usual. Looked a bit on the seedy-side, but I reckon she'll live till you see her tonight. Eeh, love's young dream . . . it seems to have addled what bits of brains you had.'

CHAPTER 10

The police didn't do house-to-house in Unthank till the Friday evening; they'd left Pottyville till last. Sergeant Dudley in his Panda; two plainclothes men from Penrith in an unmarked car. The police helicopter was still blatting overhead occasionally, but they were mainly combing the fells to the south, towards Kirkby Stephen.

Sergeant Dudley caught Ralph and Ruby at the cottage gate; he'd not shaved very well; there was a little line of bristles across his cheek, that looked like a scar. His shirt wasn't all that clean where it met his neck, and he looked absolutely whacked.

'Well, kids, what do *you* know about Postie?'

Ruby gave a horrible nervous start, then said hurriedly, 'I was on the half-past-seven bus to Penrith. I never saw nothing.'

'I know you were, my love,' said Sergeant Dudley, consulting his notebook; his voice got gentler, as he got tireder. 'So what you so nervous about, Ruby?'

'Well, they might come back an' grab somebody else,' said Ruby, defiantly.

'I don't think they're after what you've got, Ruby!'

Ruby bridled crossly, but she still looked a nervous wreck.

'What about you, young feller-me-lad?'

Ralph jumped, in his turn; he'd almost fallen asleep on his feet. 'I met Postie that morning – he stopped to have a word wi' me. That was before he went to our post-office . . .' He wasn't scared of Sergeant Dudley; you can't be scared of two things at once. He felt rather sorry for Sergeant Dudley . . . but best tell him the truth as near as possible. Villages were full of nosy eyes; nothing escaped unseen.

Sergeant Dudley consulted his notebook again. 'Yeah, Mrs Norton noticed you talking to him . . . what about?'

'He had a new dirty joke he wanted to tell me,' said Ralph. Somehow, being dead tired made lying easier; that and not caring much if you were found out or not. In some ways, it would be a comfort to be locked up in Penrith police-station. Except the dog-things could cut through walls . . .

'Mrs Norton said you gave Postie something, Ralph?' Dudley's weary eyes were still terribly sharp. Ralph, caught out, gaped and blushed helplessly . . . Sergeant Dudley's eyes widened at the blush, and Ralph thought it was all up. But Dudley just said, shrewdly:

'Dirty postcard was it, Ralph? One of Postie's Port Said Specials?'

Ralph had the sense to lower his head and shuffle. Dudley grinned, man-to-man.

'What's a Port Said Special?' asked Ruby, wide-eyed.

'Never you mind, Miss. What were you doing out on the road, that time o' morning, Ralph?' But Ralph had an answer for that one.

'Todd's hens were making a racket. Thought mebbe that dog had come back.'

'You got dogs on the bloody brain, son . . .'

'Have you found any sign of its body?' Ralph couldn't leave it alone.

'Son, I've got more to do than worry about dead dogs. That van had registered packets aboard worth five thousand quid. We'll get them bastards, though. They musta known what way Postie went, on his rounds – that means local knowledge. And the roads are nearly empty, that time o' morning. *Somebody*'ll have seen them – they'll have made *some* mistake . . .' But he'd said that too often already, to cheer himself up. He sounded like a bored child, parroting the Lord's Prayer.

'Your Mam in?'

'Yeah.' Sergeant Dudley limped sore-footed up the garden path. For the first time, Ralph noticed white hairs among the ginger fringe that hung below the back of his cap. He was probably hoping Mam would give him a cup of tea. A great wave of pity for Sergeant Dudley swept over Ralph. These great waves of pity seemed to come, when you hadn't been to bed for two nights . . .

'Let's go to the hayloft,' said Ruby, suddenly shivering. Ralph picked up the shotgun; it seemed to weigh a ton. He'd spent the last two nights sitting fully-clothed at his bedroom window, with the shotgun resting on the sill. It was the best place, at night. At least it was upstairs, and gave a good view of Ruby's window, across the gardens. And he could just see the kennel in Jack Norton's yard, and hear Nance and Jet stirring and scratching in the stillness of the night. If the dog-things came, Nance and Jet'd know . . . *they'd* give warning.

66

Ruby had been sitting up too. They both had torches, and flashed signals to each other. One long flash for 'I'm OK'. Three quick flashes for trouble.

There'd been no trouble; but the harvest-moon had been full and bright, and Ralph had died a hundred deaths as shadows seemed to move. Or when he dozed, and came awake with a gaping, gasping, half-paralysed leap, knowing the dog-things could have taken him a hundred times over as he slept. The panic, till Ruby answered his torch-flash . . .

They couldn't go without real sleep much longer. Ruby had been told off three times for dozing over the check-out. Ralph was more used to it; he sometimes had to stay up four nights on the trot, during the lambing-season. But this non-stop being afraid was making his mind *float*.

Having policemen in the village made you feel a bit safer; and the chopper overhead. But not much. The dog-things could take the chopper just like *that*, clean out of the air. If they wanted to . . .

They huddled in the darkness of Jack Norton's hayloft. No safety here, either. They ought to be out in the open, under people's eyes . . . but they huddled in the dark just the same. Below, a sick cow, kept shut in, rattled her chain and mooed mournfully, like a bovine ghost.

'Three days an' they haven't found him,' whispered Ruby, pulling Ralph's arm tight around her, like it was a scarf. It was the fourth time she'd said it already, and she was starting to get on his nerves.

'They won't find him now,' he said.

'What about his van, an' that poor little dog?'

'Look – they took away three yards of GPO wall at Penrith – solid foot-thick concrete. A van an' dog is *nothing*!' He heard his voice rising to that hated squeak.

'What you think they done wi' Postie?'

'I'll soon know – they'll come for me next. I don't know why they haven't come already . . .'

'Oh, Ralph, don't say that.' She buried her face in his anorak. 'They're frightened of being seen . . . the police . . . the helicopter.'

'They weren't frightened of being seen at Penrith GPO . . . they musta been *desperate* for them eggs.'

'Mebbe they've gone, now they got those eggs. I haven't felt them since . . . in me head. Have you?' She was groping for hope.

'Yes,' he said. 'But very faint.' He had to be honest. 'They'll lie low till the police have gone. Then they'll come.'

'I've felt them too . . . faint. I just keep trying to kid meself it's my imagination.'

'They're just getting cleverer at hiding . . .'

'Oh, Ralph, what do they *want*? I keep on thinking about . . . werewolves . . .'

He could tell she was going to cry any minute. And there was nothing to comfort her with.

'I think . . . they've been coming to earth a long, long time. People in the old days saw them sometimes, and that's how the werewolf story started. An' now they want Prepoc. Every time I open that coffin, they come. But not straight away. If they'd come straight away, they'd have got you an' me, instead of Postie an' the GPO at Penrith . . .'

He could feel her starting to sob, deep inside. Trying to stop herself. Deep, catchy, heaving breaths, shaking her thin back under his arm. But he had to work it out, get it straight. And he could only do it by talking to *her*.

'Mebbe every time the coffin's opened, it sends some sort of signal. There's a sort of aerial. Maybe they're far out in space most of the time, an' when they get the signal, it takes them a bit to get here . . .'

'But how did they know where the eggs had gone? How did they find Postie's van an' the GPO?'

'I don't know, Ruby, I don't *know*. Maybe the eggs were radioactive, and they can trace them wi' some kind of Geiger counter. But I don't *know*.'

'If they want Prepoc, why don't they just take the coffin an' leave us alone?'

'Mebbe they can't find the coffin when it's shut. Maybe the lid's radiation-proof.'

'Oh, Ralph, I was so happy with you. I wanted us to get married . . .'

Then the sobs really came. Ralph held her, awkwardly, and a slow sullen rage filled him, as she cried. Finally he said:

'I know one thing – I'm not tekkin' much more o' this. I'm not hangin' around waitin' for them to come for me, like a sheep waitin' to be slaughtered. I'm goin' to . . .'

'What, Ralph?' She stopped sobbing abruptly, and lifted her head off his chest, staring at him, wet-faced.

'I'm goin' to kill them, Ruby. Me Mam killed one – she nearly blew its whole head off. They're not immortal gods. I touched one – it was really *dead* . . .'

'But Ralph, you never killed nothing. You can't even bear to kill a rabbit . . .'

'Yes I have . . . *crows*! They're not fit to live . . . like crows. *Vermin*. Vermin, vermin, *vermin*.'

As if vermin was a magic word, a torrent of black hate flowed through him, such as he'd never felt in his life. It made him feel strong. Not wet and wobbly, like he'd felt the last three days.

'But Ralph, what with? You only got two cartridges . . .'

'Prepoc's gotta gun up there . . . it takes great lumps out of things . . . just like theirs do. An' he's got two helmets . . . I put one on . . . it made me into Prepoc, somehow.' He told her about the fun-helmet. 'Mebbe the black one's his fighting-helmet. Mebbe it'll make me fight like Prepoc. Show me how to do it.'

'But Ralph, you can't go up there again, alone. They'd get you straight away . . . it's what they're waiting for. Then I'll never see you again.' She clung to him. 'Don't go!'

'If I wait here, they'll get me anyway. I can't sleep. I'd rather be *dead* than this. If only the fell wasn't so empty . . .'

'It won't be – Sunday.' She'd suddenly stopped crying, altogether.

'Wotcher mean?'

'Don't you remember? First Sunday in August?' She was actually teasing him, smiling faintly as if in triumph.

'*What?*'

'Hikers! The Ten Fells Walk. There'll be hundreds of them, all the way up to the cairn.'

'Cle-ver girl. So if I go up in the middle of them . . .'

'*We* go up,' she said quietly. 'Both of us.'

'Ruby, you mustn't risk yourself. There's no point . . .'

'Try and stop me, Ralph Edwards.' Her face was strangely changed, in the faint light from the wood-slatted, cobwebby window. Set and determined. Her eyes had a shining look he couldn't bear to look at for long.

'They take you, Ralph Edwards, they might as well take me too. And don't try sneaking off without me. I'll be watching.'

'Ruby . . .'

'Give us a kiss – it makes me feel braver.'

*

Sundays in August were a day of dread to the people of Unthank. Most Sundays they gave themselves a lie-in, except the faithful few who went to church. Even the cows were milked a bit late.

But Sundays in August, they were awakened by the chimes of ice-cream vans at eight. By nine, the smell of hotdogs and hamburgers came floating through open windows, spoiling their appetite for bacon and eggs. Then it was the great ten-wheeled pleasure-coaches; trying to turn on the tiny village green; churning up the grass; knocking down the railings round the tiny, marble war-memorial; grating their chrome and gleaming red, blue and gold paintwork against the corners of the old, grey, limestone houses. Transistors blaring out Radio One, quite drowning out the morning service on Radio Four. Rows of people in bobble-caps, sitting on front-garden walls, dropping lolly-sticks and hamburger wrappers among the old-fashioned dahlias and London Pride. Dogs running wild and barking, peeing on garden-gnomes and cocking up their legs against the sundial in the little churchyard, while the village hens and cattle, safely locked away for the morning, cackled and mooed and moved uneasily in their pens.

Every window in the village had a lace curtain that day, even if it didn't normally. Crowds of strangers gathered, discussing loudly the architecture of the houses, the state of the vegetables in the gardens, the amount of incest among families living in such a cut-off spot. They hammered on the door of the little sub-post office, demanding sweets and soft-drinks, and would not go away; the postmistress always went to spend those Sundays with her sister in Ravensbeck. Other hikers knocked at the doors of houses, demanding to use the toilet, then going off and peeing practically anywhere, when nobody answered.

The villagers were a whole week clearing up afterwards; and still a lot of animals cut their feet on broken glass.

Then, at about ten o'clock, a tannoy-van would start bellowing routes and grid-references; there would be yelled wisecracks and ribald cheers, and the sound of many booted feet moving off, and silence would fall, until the evening. When it happened all over again.

Ralph and Ruby launched themselves into the middle of the upward-surging wave. Having made up their minds to die in battle, they had both managed a decent night's sleep, and felt dozy and soggy as a result. Ralph was carrying the inevitable shotgun; several

70

officious middle-aged men asked him if he had a licence for it. Ruby had never seen Ralph so rude and glowering . . .

Within a quarter of a mile, the wave began to leave its flotsam. Three rather fat ladies, in shorts that creased and bulged, sitting holding up legs already over-pink with the sun, and taking off their boots to look for imaginary stones. A group of fed-up teenagers with a vicar in charge; who had made them sit in a circle and was intoning in a loud and embarrassing voice:

'I will lift up mine eyes unto the hills; from whence cometh my help?'

There was even a wild-eyed bearded man with a sandwich-board, which declaimed on one side, 'FLEE FROM THE WRATH TO COME' and on the other, 'YOUR ADVERSARY THE DEVIL GOETH ABOUT AS A ROARING LION SEEKING WHOM HE MAY DEVOUR.'

'If he sees one of our dog-friends,' said Ralph bitterly, 'it'll *really* make his day.'

They got safely up to the cairn, careful to stay right in the middle of the slowly moving horde, and settled to wait. The cairn was like a fairground. Some enthusiasts had even set up a folding table and were selling membership of the National Trust and the Ramblers' Association. The tide of litter spread outwards from the cairn, like foam around a sea-girt rock, and began to blow southwards across the heather in a merry skipping flock of crisp-bags.

And yet, just as suddenly, the fairground departed, towards the next distant cairn, giggling and shouting as it went. The Ramblers' Association lot were the last to go. As they folded up their table, they discovered that Ralph and Ruby were actual local yokels; they began asking their views, as farmworkers, on the establishment of rights-of-way for walkers . . .

Ralph grew uncomfortably aware that one cairn, one folding table, two local yokels and three members of the Ramblers' Association were an ideal-size mouthful for the device that had removed three yards of concrete from the GPO wall at Penrith . . . He eyed the one decent-sized cloud in the sky, waited until it had drifted across the sun, and then announced, as a local yokel:

'Goin' to be a rare old thunderstorm in half an hour.'

The ramblers eyed the cloud with him, got their anoraks out of their rucksacks, and went on asking about the life of the working countryside . . .

'Let's make a start clearing up the litter, Ralph,' said Ruby suddenly, with a glint in her eye. Taking up the cue, Ralph said to the ramblers:

'Like to help? We'll be on all day otherwise.' They both began frantically grabbing up handfuls of plastic cups and crisp-bags . . .

The ramblers turned their eyes back to the one sizeable cloud, which by this time had drifted quite clear of the sun and was notably diminishing in size. 'Sorry – we must get our literature back to the car, before it gets wet.' They picked up their folding table and went off down the fell like the clappers.

Silence; just a slight breeze stirring the greaseproof wrappers, and the whisper of polythene bags unfolding in the bright sunlight. And a thin wisp of smoke where a discarded pop-bottle was focusing the sun's rays on a piece of dead, dry heather . . .

And then the air began to fall apart . . .

They demolished the side of the cairn in a crazy rush; Ralph pulled away two stones at the base, and the whole lot fell down. He yanked open the coffin, bobbed a little apology to the body of Prepoc, and jammed the black helmet on to his head.

CHAPTER 11

Ralph stood so still, for so long, that Ruby grew afraid he'd been turned to stone, or was dead and still standing up or something . . .

'Ralph,' she yelled, 'Ralph.' Grabbed his anorak and shook him. But she might as well have been shaking a statue. He swayed a bit, but otherwise there was no response. *'Ralph!'*

Then he dropped into a crouch, his knuckles nearly touching the ground. Almost like an animal dropping back on to four legs. He never gave her a glance, but stared hard, first east towards the distant hikers, then north, then west. Then he reached quickly into the coffin and picked up the red egg, and opened it with a deft twist, like he'd done it hundreds of times before. Took an expertly measured dab on his fingertip, and thrust it up inside the visor of the helmet to his mouth. From inside the helmet came the sound of licking . . . Then he picked up the long, black, metal shape that Ruby knew was Prepoc's gun, and checked it over swiftly with professional skill. Ruby thought she heard a faint hiss of displeasure inside the black helmet . . . All his movements were so smooth, sinuous . . . not Ralph's slow steady plodding at all.

She knew with terrible certainty that whatever was hidden within the helmet it was no longer Ralph.

Then it turned and looked at her; the visor of the helmet reflected the light, like them posh sunglasses; she saw a funny, moony reflection of her own face, and the sky behind. Nothing else. Then the creature took her arm and twisted it cleverly. It didn't hurt, but the next second she was lying on her face.

'Ralph,' she screamed, though she knew it was quite useless. Ralph wasn't there any more . . .

Then the creature dropped down beside her, and began to lead her away from the cairn, crawling along a slight dip in the ground. She tried to struggle, but it was far too strong. After about forty yards, the creature made another faint noise, perhaps of satisfaction, almost like a short, rough purr. Then it pressed her flat to the heather, and whispered:

'Wait . . . five minutes. Then close the coffin . . . rebuild the cairn . . . take shotgun . . . go home.' It was hard to understand it; it was using Ralph's mouth, but not in Ralph's way. Its voice was full of th's and f's and hisses.

Then it was gone, running crouched low to the heather, using the hand that did not hold the gun to keep balance. Once, it paused, then suddenly leapt to the right. Sometimes it crawled, incredibly fast. It was sinuous, like a snake, or, she thought with a shudder, like a cat on the hunt, belly pressed to the ground. A cat inside Ralph's trousers and anorak . . .

It was all too weird to bear. She pressed her face into the heather and wept and wept, and wished she was dead. She must have fallen into some kind of sleep or daze. She wakened with a start; she thought she'd heard a short, sharp bang, somewhere off south, that had awakened her; but she couldn't be sure. Its echoes seemed to be still ringing around the hillside.

Listlessly, she closed the coffin, and rebuilt the cairn. It was what the creature had told her to do; it was what Ralph would have wanted. The stones kept falling down again, and hurting her hands; she felt like screaming her head off; but she knew that if she started that, she'd never be able to stop.

Tiny tentacles inside the helmet uncurled, felt for Ralph's ears and eyes and nose and mouth. He didn't struggle this time; perhaps because he could still see the cairn and the fellside, through the visor of the helmet. And then . . .

It was almost as if his body was a motorcar, and his mind was driving it, and then Prepoc opened the car door and pushed Ralph across into the passenger-seat, and began to drive the car himself. That was the way Ralph explained it later, to Ruby . . .

Prepoc was not pleased with the body he had acquired; he thought it weak and stiff-backed and slow. Hardly any sense of smell; half-deaf. Only Ralph's eyes was he pleased with, that they could see so many sharp details. He was quite delighted with Ralph's eyes . . .

Prepoc's first action was to find the enemy; using the helmet he picked them up easily, one east, one north, one west, well back in an encircling ring . . . Prepoc was deeply disappointed to find they were merely 'Wawaka' – the sound of the name, Ralph thought, was oddly like a dog's barking. Or how a dog's barking might seem to a cat . . .

Prepoc did not think much of Wawaka as warriors. Unreliable as allies, and easy prey as enemies. Brave, but far too excitable; acting before they had thought. With a fatal trick of bunching together in a pack when they were angry or frightened in war . . . With luck, he might kill all three with one shot. It was a matter of pride with Prepoc, to kill all three with one shot. Otherwise, there was no achievement in killing Wawaka at all . . .

But should the Wawaka *be* killed; were they legitimate prey? Had they committed a crime? Yes – the crime of *nithila* – world-breaking. Entering the planet of another species unlawfully, without permission of the council. Intending to take members of another species captive for their own purpose. Death was the penalty for *nithila*. They *were* legitimate prey. The red joy of hunting filled Prepoc's mind. Ralph thought it odd, Prepoc using all these strange words, and yet he could understand him perfectly . . . must be because they were occupying the same mind . . .

Prepoc bent and took some of the paste from the red egg on to his tongue. Suddenly Ralph felt he understood all things. The growing and diminishing of clouds; the whirls of hot air rising from the hot land and twisting and shaping the clouds. The joyful mind-twitter of the white gulls, circling on the thermals so far overhead . . . The ticking of every insect on every leaf; the old fox chewing a dead vole with enjoyment, concealed in the bed of a nearby burn. Even the group-minds of the sheep beyond the crest of the fell, where they had fled in terror from the noise of the hikers and their radios.

But above all, he felt the minds of the Wawaka in their encircling ring. Except the ring was moving away, very fast. The Wawaka were frightened now; frightened of the red war-song of Prepoc that was echoing and echoing inside the helmet. They were fleeing south, out of sight beyond the bowl of the land. Starting to bunch together. Now was the time to hunt, to rid the earth of them, the slinking black stains . . .

But first this ape-female must be got to a place of safety. She was confused, frightened. She must be told what to do for her own safety. Prepoc dragged Ruby away, left her lying sobbing on her face. Ralph felt detached, unconcerned. What could *he* do? Prepoc was in control . . . the important thing was the Wawaka. Ralph felt Prepoc slip the red egg into an anorak pocket, and they were away, moving low and alarmingly fast. But all Ralph felt was Prepoc's hunting-glee; he let it flood his mind; it was most enjoyable.

And yet, along with the red hunting-joy, Prepoc felt great love and care. For the innocent things. For the small, blue butterflies that fluttered up from the heather beneath his feet. For the white scuts of rabbits, as they bounded away in alarm. For the smallest wild flower that blew in the wind. Even for the dry, dying blades of grass. Nothing else must die, when the Wawaka died; no harmless thing. The Wawaka must be trapped in some barren, rocky place. And even that was sad, for the rocks themselves had life and being, of a slow, ticking, centuries-long sort. Even the rocks were sacred . . .

And still the Wawaka retreated; and still they bunched closer to each other, bewildered by the change that had taken place in Ralph, baffled by the dreadful cat-warrior that had appeared from nowhere. Stupid Wawaka, three strong bodies and only one hysterical pack-mind between them . . .

Then, in their desperation, they tried a crude ambush, as the fell-top crags began to narrow into a funnelling valley. Wawaka, Prepoc thought, never learnt a thing . . . same old tricks. Still . . .

Well back out of sight, Prepoc used his blaster to stun a small flock of sheep. He took the stiff-legged leading ewe where she lay, and smeared a little green paste from the red egg on to her fleece. The stunning did not last long; the sheep revived and began to flee up the funnelling valley towards the Wawaka, away from the frightening black-helmeted creature.

Prepoc's conscience smote him, that perhaps he drove the sheep to their death. But it was *metheht* – a legal military stratagem in a just war. To be balanced against the damage three crazed Wawaka could do this planet. And if he acted swiftly enough, he might still save the sheep . . .

He sensed the Wawaka become aware of the radioactive paste on the sheep, tremble with excitement as they approached, tighten their fingers round the triggers of their blasters . . . Blind to everything but the paste, they didn't sense Prepoc slipping away to the right in a low crouching circle until he came out on top of the crags, above and behind them. The sheep had stopped to graze, getting over their fright, and the Wawaka were creeping their way down towards them.

Patiently, Prepoc lined them up in his telescopic sight, waiting for them to come into line, so he could take them all in one blast . . .

But they were slow coming into line. Prepoc moved this way and that . . . and then fired.

At the last moment, in the moment of firing, one Wawaka slipped on a piece of loose scree and fell. Fell behind the others.

It was as if someone had taken a delicate chisel. The tiniest scoop of rock vanished, and two black Wawaka with it. But the next moment the third Wawaka was up and running like a hunted hare. Prepoc got him in his sight again. But the small flock of sheep were in the way. Then there was a grouse and her chicks that must not be harmed. Then it was rabbits. From living thing to living thing, the Wawaka ran cunningly; but nothing but Wawaka would Prepoc kill. The Wawaka vanished over the crest of the land. In bitter disgust at himself, Prepoc took another finger-full of paste. And followed.

It was Ralph's body that failed in the end, worn out with the great leaps that Prepoc demanded of it, in spite of the green paste. On one piece of crag, he leapt and missed his handhold and fell. And in the falling, the helmet came off . . .

And suddenly it was just Ralph lying there, hardly able to put one leg in front of another for weariness, and very far from home.

He never knew how he made it back to the cairn; he took several more spots of the green paste, but they hardly worked at all, now. Ruby had gone; but she'd repaired the cairn as best she could. It looked rough, but it would have to do . . .

Ralph hovered piteously, the helmet in one hand, the blaster in the other. Without the helmet, he didn't know where the last Wawaka was; it might be watching now, lining him up. But if Ralph put on the helmet, he would become Prepoc, and the dreadful chase would start all over again.

At least the air wasn't falling apart . . . He staggered down the fell, carrying the helmet in one hand, the blaster in the other. If the air did start to fall apart, he was ready for it.

But all the way down to the road, there was no sign of the last Wawaka. The biggest fright he got was from a tripper-bus, that almost ran him down as he blundered wearily out on to the road without looking both ways. The driver blared his horn angrily; the bus missed him by inches, and kids gazing out of the back window hooted and put up two fingers at him, and stared at the strange objects he was carrying.

Below the road, the usual odd change took place; he worried less and less about the Wawaka, and more what Mam would say about the state of his clothes. He must find somewhere to hide the helmet and blaster . . . somewhere close to home.

The whole hillside was pocked with old lead-mines, and Ralph knew them all. The lowest was in a tiny crag that served as the top wall of Jack Norton's bottom field. Ralph had only found it one day by chance, desperate for shelter from a sudden summer downpour. Two small ash-trees grew from a cleft. Between and behind them there was a sideways slit in the rock, no bigger than a child's coffin stood on end. And well hidden by a mass of bracken. Maybe the Romans had made it; Romans had always been after lead and silver in these parts. Ralph had kept it as his secret; he hadn't even showed it to Ruby yet.

And maybe the lead in the rocks would mask the radiation that came from Prepoc's things . . .

He crawled in, aching-boned; he only just managed to force the helmet through; scraped the black paint a bit. But the mine opened out quite a lot, once you were inside. Pitch-black, of course, after ten yards. And if you didn't watch, you could give your head a nasty bang on an outcrop. But somebody had once smoothed the floor, and Ralph knew it by feel, every inch of the way. Fifty feet down, he stowed the helmet, egg and blaster safe in the deepest crevice.

Well, that was done. For the first time for hours, he felt in control of things. He crept back nearly to the entrance, where it was light, and sat down. It was bone dry and cool; cool after the heat of the day. He could relax. What a day! He massaged his aching legs with his hands. And realized to his horror that he'd ripped both knees out of his best Sunday jeans. And the Polish boots . . . the ones Mam called rubbish . . . were starting to tear apart. The tops were coming away from the soles. Prepoc had done it . . . but Mam would kill *him*.

It was too much. He was ravenously hungry, dying of thirst, only wanted his bed . . . but he couldn't face Mam's fury. He'd just give himself five minutes . . . it was cool here, peaceful . . .

He put his head on his arm and slept.

He wakened, aching worse than ever. Didn't know how long he'd slept. But he had an awful feeling of being too late for something. Suppose the Wawaka had come looking for him? Suppose it had come for Ruby? What had it done to the village? Frantic, he scrambled out into the daylight.

The sun was setting, behind the distant peaks of the Lake District, dropping between Skiddaw and Saddleback. The whole village lay below him. As he watched, Jack Norton came out of his house, to his car. Going down to the pub at Melmerby. Every lazy line of Jack's body, as he leaned against the bonnet to light his pipe, said all was well. Mrs Thompson, fresh from Evensong, was at the churchyard gate, talking to Mrs Rowley about God or altar-flowers or cleaning the church brasses. Mam came out into the garden and fiercely snatched from the washing-line three pairs of her own blue washed-out knickers, her mouth full of pegs. He looked at Ruby's bedroom window, and there was Ruby leaning out on the sill, reading some woman's magazine. As he watched, she looked up and scanned the hillside anxiously. Watching for *him* . . .

All was well.

With a great surge of gladness, he began to stagger down the sloping turf. His knees ached abominably. Ruby saw him and waved, and he waved back . . .

Then blackness hit him, and he knew nothing.

CHAPTER 12

Someone threw him roughly on to a gridded metal floor. He felt the grid on his cheek; its coldness, vibration. Then it seemed to him he bounced; like a rubber ball. Felt himself curving upwards into the air. His bottom hit a rounded metal ceiling, and he bounced downwards again. Now he was turning over and over. His knee hit something sharp and he flew off in another direction. He'd had some funny dreams in his time; but dreams never *hurt*. I mean, vampires might bury their fangs in your throat; but you never felt nothing . . .

To break up this awful dream, he opened his eyes, and saw a row of metal pipes drifting past, with a small wheel sticking out. He grabbed the wheel one-handed, and the rest of his body swung round and banged against the pipes painfully, then began to bounce back the other way. He swung to and fro wildly, like a pendulum, and began to feel very sick. He grabbed the pipes with his other hand, and strained to get his body braced and still. But behind him his legs were still swinging, like a dog wagging its tail. He drew them in to his body, and braced his knees against the pipes as well. Then got the conviction he was not braced against a wall at all, but kneeling on a floor.

Hanging on grimly, he stared about. The room he was in was immensely tall and narrow, like a skyscraper; with a row of doors set up one wall. Except the doors were not tall, like ordinary doors, but very wide and low; with their hinges along the top, and handles at the bottom . . .

Except where *was* top and where *was* bottom? His stomach didn't seem to know. All the food he'd ever eaten seemed to be crowding up into his throat, like an audience trying to force its way out of a burning cinema. He gulped to ease the pain, and immediately his mouth became so full of food he couldn't breathe. The liquid food began trickling up his nostrils, burning them. He opened his mouth and a great jet of food shot out and hit the wall. Some of it stuck to the wall, looking revolting. The rest bounced back, coming straight

80

at his head. He ducked instinctively and it passed over his shoulder. Hit the far wall, left a bit more of itself, and came bouncing back again, but slower now.

Then it stopped altogether and hung in the middle of the room, and slowly shaped itself into a perfect, shiny, grey-green ball, surrounded by several smaller balls that hung round it, then slowly fell back into it, one by one. The big ball swallowed them with a kind of hiccup that left it trembling for several seconds. Then it was still. Then it slowly, slowly, began to drift back towards him . . .

He thought wildly that he'd seen something like this before . . . on the telly. Some science-fiction movie? No . . . my God, the games astronauts used to play with pens and pencils in Apollo Fifteen . . . games with weightlessness.

He was in space.

The one sane thought he had was that he must get down to the floor. But which *was* the floor? All the walls were cluttered with doors, handles, pipes. Except one, which was all metal grid. That must be the floor. He pushed himself out towards it. Travelling at frightening speed, he hit it with a thump, and bounced . . .

Finally, he managed to get hold of the floor by thrusting his fingers hard through the metal grid. Its edges were sharp and painful; blood welled out of a cut in his finger and immediately formed a little ball that clung there, growing bigger, till it was as big as a pea. Then a wrinkly skin seemed to grow over it, as the finger stopped bleeding.

Then, as he hung there, he heard the whine, the rusty rumble of machinery. The whole ship began to rock like a boat in a heavy sea. Then it slowly turned right over. He felt sick again, but he had nothing left to be sick with. Over and over the ship turned . . .

And then everything got better. The turning settled down; the sense of weightlessness left him. The floor truly became the floor, and he could walk without holding on; though his weight seemed only about a tenth of what it usually was.

Suddenly he understood: advanced space vessels, he'd been taught at school, would turn slowly on their own axis, to give some illusion of gravity. Though he had a shrewd idea that this particular advanced spaceship wasn't in very good nick. It didn't revolve all the time; only when they could get it to work . . . It gave him a slight contempt for the vessel's crew, that was nearly as good as courage . . .

He saw that the room wasn't really tall like a skyscraper, but a long corridor, with a row of perfectly ordinary doors running along one side.

Each door had a little star-symbol below its round window . . .

Then he knew who held him prisoner.

He shook with terror; he shook for a long time, but eventually the shaking stopped. He decided he'd rather be dead than have one of them touch him. But you couldn't be dead by wishing it . . .

A weapon. He must have a weapon. If he fought them, they might kill him quickly . . . that would be best. He knew he was thinking insanely; but who could be sane *here*? And the insanity of fighting and being killed was better than the insanity of letting them *touch* him. He looked round wildly. Spanners? Levers? A fire-extinguisher? Anything to make a weapon . . .

But there was nothing. Only the row of doors.

Perhaps the doors were cupboards? Perhaps they held weapons? He looked through the round window set in the first door. But it was misted over with some grey, powdery stuff. He put a hand on the handle, then hesitated. Perhaps one of them would be behind the door?

But they'd come soon anyway . . . he turned the handle and pulled the door open.

It was a metal cupboard, about six feet high and three deep. There were metal straps set in the back wall, a bit like suitcase handles but set horizontally. One at the level of his head, two wide apart lower down, and two wide apart just above the floor.

On one side, cylinders hung on racks, with meaningless dials and long, disconnected tubes dangling, made of something like polythene. They looked abandoned, left over, disused.

On the floor below grew mould. Great wheel-like patterns of mould, like the sort you found on old bread, but much bigger. They spread across the floor, bigger than dinner plates and three inches thick, with circular bands of yellow, blue and purple, but mainly grey. The mould was growing over heaps of something lying on the floor; he couldn't make out what it was. It could have been *anything*, from decayed fruit to dog-dirt.

The moulds seemed to be fighting each other, eating each other, one wheel cutting savagely into another, with little drops of liquid like honey standing out on top, here and there. The stench was appalling. He had a feeling even the moulds were dying . . .

He slammed the door, feeling a little more contempt; remembering

Mam's disgust at finding even a *speck* of mould on an old jar of jam; the way her nose wrinkled; the way she threw it straight out. Mould to Mam was bad housekeeping, inefficiency, stupidity. It made Ralph begin to despise the Wawaka. If they lived in such a hopeless pigsty, they couldn't be very efficient . . .

So he opened the next cupboard-door with a little more confidence. The same stench met him. The same set-up; disconnected tubes. The only difference was that the stuff on the floor, under the mould, had more shape. It looked like a few . . . bones. He reached down to touch one; then something warned him not to. Instead, he pulled a Biro out of his pocket and touched the biggest bone with that. The moment he touched it, it flaked apart in thin, grey slivers, like dried-out clay; no strength left in it.

It looked like the bone out of a shoulder of mutton, when Mam had carved the last sliver of meat off it.

This must be the Wawaka's deep-freeze food-store, only it had broken down. No chance of a weapon here.

So he opened the next cupboard rather hopelessly. The shock of what he saw brought him jolting upright.

There was a rib-cage lying on the floor; the mould was all over it, but it was definitely a rib-cage. Of some man-size animal that had walked upright. And more long bones. And something solid, lying in a shadowed corner, that could only be a skull . . . He slammed the door shut, gagging on his own bile. He was in the spaceship mortuary, containing their dead from space-wars, to be taken home and buried at the end of their voyage. Funny, the Cats had buried Prepoc on Earth . . . and Prepoc hadn't decayed . . . the Cats must be more efficient at funerals.

He didn't want to look in any more cupboards, but some dreadful curiosity drove him on.

The next cupboard contained a skeleton, upright; held up against the rear wall by the metal straps. You could see it was still joined together by strips of muscle, under the mould. And from the metal cylinders on the wall, pipes still led down into it. And even under the mould, he could tell it was not the skeleton of a Wawaka.

It was a human skeleton.

He slammed the door quickly; too quickly. It shook the whole cupboard, and he heard things falling to the floor inside . . .

His mind seized up. He stood clenching and unclenching his hands desperately, not knowing what to do. And while he was still standing like that, the well-kicked metal door at the far end of the corridor was pushed open. His heart gave a dreadful leap, like it was trying to leave his body through his throat.

But the dog that came through was quite a small dog, no bigger than a terrier. A brown mongrel with soft floppy ears and a friendly expression, and its tongue hanging slightly out. Even in his panic, Ralph was struck by how healthy it looked. Its eyes were very bright and lively, its coat sleek and smooth and freshly groomed, and it was as plump as a dog can be, without being unhealthy. It wore a silver collar and medallion . . .

And the medallion was star-shaped . . .

When it saw Ralph, it gave a short bark of recognition, and ran up to him, wagging its tail.

'What do you *want?*' shouted Ralph, clenching his fists. The dog looked baffled and upset by this unfriendly welcome. Its ears drooped, its tail stopped wagging. It looked forlorn; whined in a familiar way.

For some reason, Ralph knew suddenly it was an ordinary earth-dog. Very far from home, but definitely an ordinary earth-dog. In fact, he thought he'd seen it before . . . Then he knew.

It was Maisie. Postie's dog. Only she looked so sleek and fit he hadn't recognized her.

'Maisie!' She flew to him with joyous barks. Flung herself into his arms, licking him with a passion of recognition. For a moment, he forgot all his troubles, in the joy of finding something he knew.

Then Maisie, by polite wriggling, asked to be put down.

He put her down. She ran to the second last cupboard in the row; looked back at him and whined pleadingly, one paw held in the air.

She wanted him to open that door . . .

He walked towards her, one dreadful thought filling his mind. But perhaps she only wanted something to eat . . . his mind blanked out on the unthinkable. He stopped half-way to that door.

'Come here, Maisie!' he said sharply. But still she stood there and whined, paw uplifted. In desperation he went across to pick her up again, and bring her away.

But as he stooped to pick her up, with his head close to that door, he distinctly heard a human voice. Heard it say:

'Oh my God, oh my God, oh my God!' over and over again. Like the voice on a worn-out gramophone record, stuck in a groove.

And he knew the voice. Postie's voice.

The voice stopped. There was a slight creaking inside the cupboard. Then it started again.

'Oh my God, oh my God, oh my God!'

Maisie whined pleadingly and clawed at the door.

'Oh no,' said Ralph. 'Please, Maisie, no!'

Then through the door, Postie's voice said:

'Who's that? Is that you, Ralph? For God's sake get me out of here.'

Then Ralph had to open the door. Maisie, at his feet, barked wildly. But she wouldn't go in. And neither would Ralph.

Postie was fastened to the back wall of the cupboard, his neck and wrists and ankles held cruciform by metal strips.

He still wore his Post Office trousers, with the thin red stripe, though one leg had been cut roughly away. He still wore his old khaki Post Office coat, with the official metal badge pinned to his lapel. But tubes led down from the cylinders and dials, into Postie's bare leg and up one of his nostrils. Half his ginger hair had been shaved off, and a metal plate was taped to his bare skull, with wires leading up to the dials.

But that wasn't the worst. The grey and purple mould was climbing up his naked leg; and the right side of his face was covered with it, even the constantly blinking eye.

But the other clear blue eye was Postie's still.

'God, mate, am I glad to see you! Got the police with you? Let me out of here, will you? I thought the police'd never get here . . . By, I could do wi' a mug o' your Mam's tea – a real pint-pot full. It's thinking about yer Mam an' her tea that's kept me going.' He tried to smile; the side of his face under the grey mould suddenly split from jaw to eye, and a bead of that same honey-coloured liquid formed, and ran down the mould.

'Postie,' said Ralph. He could hardly get the word out; his throat felt full of dry dust. 'Postie . . .'

Postie slumped. 'Oh, God, kid, they got you an'all . . . oh, God help us. I tried not to tell them who'd given me the parcel. But I couldn't bear it . . . not when the grey stuff began crawling up me leg . . . I told them, thinking they'd stop it. But they just left me here . . .'

'Postie . . .'

'Look, kid, got your knife on you? Finish me off, will you? I've been praying for someone to finish me off . . .'

'No, Postie, NO . . .'

85

And then the door at the end of the corridor swung open again.

And there were two of them standing there, one just behind the other. Taller than men, broader than men, black ears pricked.

Ralph just had time to notice the front one had some white hairs round his muzzle.

Then he fainted.

CHAPTER 13

This was the worst nightmare yet.

He was standing with his back pressed against a smooth wall cold as ice. The cold nibbled at his buttocks and legs; it ran up and down the knobbles of his spine, making him shiver; it invaded his lungs so he could hardly breathe; he felt he had been shivering a long time.

His head was drooping as if it weighed a ton, but it was held up by a sharp band round his throat that was almost choking him. He tried to reach up and tear the band away, but there were sharp bands round his wrists as well. He tried to move his feet, but there were more cold, sharp bands round his ankles.

He opened his eyes and saw the floor; a shiny stainless-steel floor that sloped to a drainhole in one corner . . .

He was inside one of the steel cupboards. White plastic tubes hung down around him. The left leg of his denims had been cut away; he could feel the ragged torn edge of the material against his thigh.

He was in one of the steel cupboards; like Postie. Like all the dreadful mouldy things . . . He looked for the mould, for the spreading wheels of mould.

There were none yet; that was the one thing that stopped him from screaming. No mould; yet.

Then the cupboard door swung open, and they were standing there again. They were not really like Alsatians. Their jaws were smaller, their brows higher, their eyes bigger. Both of them had a ridge of denser fur down the middle of their chests, ending in a large, wrinkled, black wart where a human navel would be. And two rows of rudimentary nipples, like the two rows of buttons on a double-breasted coat. He could see differences between them now. The leader was older, heavier. Besides the white hairs on its muzzle, it was going bald in patches, the coarse dark hair thinning on its head and arms, revealing a dull shine of dark grey skin beneath.

It reached out a long sinewy arm to Ralph's head; its fingers were nearly all bald, dark-grey wrinkled skin, with a few long black hairs on the backs of them. Ralph shut his eyes, screwed up his face, and threw his head about, trying to get away. The fingertips held him, felt like warm cracked leather. The fingers made some adjustment to a thin plastic band that ran across Ralph's head from ear to ear; immediately Ralph's head filled with high-pitched squeaking noise. The leathery warm fingers made another adjustment, then the squeaking noise became high-pitched voices, speaking queer English.

They were trying to talk to him. The thing across his ears must be some simultaneous-translation device, using computers. The squeaking was nothing like their real voices, which were all gruff and deep, growls and yaps.

The squeaking was urgent, insistent.

'Where Fefethil? Where Fefethil hiding? Fefethil who attacked us?'

In spite of his whirling terror, two things sank in with Ralph. 'Fefethil' was their name for Prepoc's people; and they were dreadfully afraid of Prepoc's people. It gave him the courage to shout:

'I'm not telling you nothing till you let me out of here. Me an' Postie as well!' His whole body was shaking, but he shouted it.

They replied; the translation-thing must work both ways.

'What you ask is pointless. The animal you call "Postie" is dying – his condition is not reversible. We cannot take him out. He'll die anyway.'

'MURDERERS!'

They went into loll-tongued grins; like Nance and Jet when they nipped the cows. Ralph's ears were filled with their crazy high-pitched squeaking. He knew it was a sort of laughter.

'Murder? You cannot *murder* an ape. Apes have no souls. You cannot murder a creature without a soul. That ape you call Postie is being used for a valid scientific experiment. Now you will answer our questions!'

'I'LL NOT!'

More insane squeaking laughter. The dark, wrinkled, leathery hand reached out again, made another slight adjustment to the thing round Ralph's ears.

Ralph's mind went suddenly and completely blank. Or rather he felt every thought was being sucked out of his mind as if by a vacuum cleaner. All draining away, like water down a plughole, till he could have screamed. Except he hadn't enough thoughts left to think of screaming.

Finally, the appalling draining feeling stopped, leaving him totally and less about the Wawaka, and more what Mam would say about the state of his clothes. He must find somewhere to hide the helmet and blaster . . . somewhere close to home.

The whole hillside was pocked with old lead-mines, and Ralph knew them all. The lowest was in a tiny crag that served as the top wall of Jack Norton's bottom field. Ralph had only found it one day by chance, desperate for shelter from a sudden summer downpour. Two small ash-trees grew from a cleft. Between and behind them there was a sideways slit in the rock, no bigger than a child's coffin stood on end. And well hidden by a mass of bracken. Maybe the Romans had made it; Romans had always been after lead and silver in these parts. Ralph had kept it as his secret; he hadn't even showed it to Ruby yet.

And maybe the lead in the rocks would mask the radiation that came from Prepoc's things . . .

He crawled in, aching-boned; he only just managed to force the helmet through; scraped the black paint a bit. But the mine opened out quite a lot, once you were inside. Pitch-black, of course, after ten yards. And if you didn't watch, you could give your head a nasty bang on an outcrop. But somebody had once smoothed the floor, and Ralph knew it by feel, every inch of the way. Fifty feet down, he stowed the helmet, egg and blaster safe in the deepest crevice.

Well, that was done. For the first time for hours, he felt in control of things. He crept back nearly to the entrance, where it was light, and sat down. It was bone dry and cool; cool after the heat of the day. He could relax. What a day! He massaged his aching legs with his hands. And realized to his horror that he'd ripped both knees out of his best Sunday jeans. And the Polish boots . . . the ones Mam called rubbish . . . were starting to tear apart. The tops were coming away from the soles. Prepoc had done it . . . but Mam would kill *him*.

It was too much. He was ravenously hungry, dying of thirst, only wanted his bed . . . but he couldn't face Mam's fury. He'd just give himself five minutes . . . it was cool here, peaceful . . .

He put his head on his arm and slept.

He wakened, aching worse than ever. Didn't know how long he'd slept. But he had an awful feeling of being too late for something. Suppose the Wawaka had come looking for him? Suppose it had

78

'You will have a chance to speak at your trial. I was addressing this young ape.'

The great Wawaka strained to break its invisible bonds. Its eyeballs rolled the more, showing yellow-brown whites all round. Its whole frame shook.

'Do not waste your strength, Wawaka!'

Then the Fefethil came into view. It was not as tall as the Wawaka, and looked frail by contrast: a graceful cheetah-like frailness that ...owed. It was grey, going paler, almost white, on the narrow chest ...d sinuous belly.

...shot out a graceful paw: pulled the wrists of the elder Wawaka ...er and fastened them with a strip of gold plastic that sparked ...ly as it joined together. The other Wawaka must have ...e same treatment, but all Ralph could see was the flash of ...spark, reflected off the steel walls of the corridor. Another, even ...voice said, 'Released'. Ralph found he could wriggle ...his face again.

...ively produced something that looked like a gold ...e two Wawaka further up the corridor with it; ...arked as it touched their black hairy bodies. ...blundered away up the corridor with bitter ...of the Fefethil were inside the cupboard ...l hoops round his neck and wrists ...ing. Ralph had never seen anything ...cat tapping a dead leaf around in ...ook the Fefethil straight in the ...ry important.

The eyes blinked at him ...sting metal staircase, ...them terrifying; but ...ws, without even ...r; and came out ...upon bank of ...e triangular ...l blue, and ...son, the

Below the road...
objects he was carr...
hooted and put up r...
bus missed him by inch...
without looking both wa...
almost ran him down as ...
Wawaka. The biggest fright...
But all the way down to th...
did start to fall apart, he was re...
carrying the helmet in one hand, ...
At least the air wasn't falling apar...
would start all over again.
put on the helmet, he would become Pre...
Wawaka was; it might be watching now, ...
the other. Without the helmet, he didn'...
Ralph hovered piteously, the helmet in on...
looked rough, but it would have to do . . .
Ruby had gone; but she'd repaired the calm as...
more spots of the green paste, but they hardly wo...
He never knew how he made it back to the calm; ...
leg in front of another for weariness, and very far from...

And suddenly it was just Ralph lying there, hardly able...
falling, the helmet came off . . .
piece of crag, he leapt and missed his handhold and fell. And
leaps that Prepoc demanded of it, in spite of the green paste. O...
It was Ralph's body that failed in the end, worn out with the gr...
followed.
disgust at himself, Prepoc took another finger-full of paste. And
kill. The Wawaka vanished over the crest of the land. In bitter
Wawaka ran cunningly; but nothing but Wawaka would Prepoc
harmed. Then it was rabbits. From living thing to living thing, the
the way. Then there was a grouse and her chicks that must not be
Prepoc got him in his sight again. But the small flock of sheep were in
moment the third Wawaka was up and running like a hunted hare.
of rock vanished, and two black Wawaka with it. But the next
It was as if someone had taken a delicate chisel. The tiniest scoop
on a piece of loose scree and fell. Fell behind the others.
At the last moment, in the moment of firing, one Wawaka slipped
that . . . and then fired.
But they were slow coming into line. Prepoc moved this way and

control-cabin seemed a squalid kennel, the doors and seats and control-panels smeared with black grease, like that patch of wall-paper by Jack Norton's kitchen door, where Nance and Jet squeezed past to sit by the fire in winter. Everything had that *scrabbled* look. The floor was covered with battered equipment and there was an overpowering smell of dog.

The Fefethil gave a hiss of disgust; then it herded the Wawaka against a vertical pipe and fastened their wrists to it, with more sparking plastic.

'Wait here,' it said to Ralph. 'They cannot harm you now.' Then, light and swift as a ghost, it was gone back downstairs.

Ralph stared out of the huge windows, trying to lose himself in the clean beauty of the cloud-patterns as they swept past. Trying not to think about Postie's split and oozing face. But he still saw Postie's face in the clouds . . .

And the Wawaka were impossible to ignore. Their bulk filled the cabin. They were both staring at him; arrogant, like black S S officers; like they were certain they'd get anything they wanted . . . He could not stare them out; he looked back out of the window, nervously.

'Ape!' said the elder. 'Do you hear me, *ape*? Listen to me, *ape*! We are injured by that Fefethil's goad – in great pain. Give us that medical box from the wall-clips above your head, *ape* – that long grey box. It contains things to ease our pain. *Ape*! Listen to me, *ape*. Do as you are told!'

Ralph would not look at them again; their eyes had power. But he could not shut out their voices; they went on and on in his brain, bullying, needling, commanding. Finally, despite all efforts to ignore them, he found himself looking at the long grey box they were talking about. It had various handles sticking out of it; its shape looked oddly familiar, though he was sure he'd never seen it before . . .

Curiously he reached up and took it down . . . it *felt* like something he had handled before . . .

Something warned him not to give it to them. But their voices went on and on in his miserable spinning brain, on and on, on and on. Finally, desperate to shut them up, he turned to hand it to them.

But the crescendo of urgency in their voices warned him just in time. They wanted it too much, for it to be just first-aid equipment. More as if it was . . .

It was a blaster; a little like Prepoc's, but shorter and stubbier and

91

neater. He snatched it away from their yearning black fingers just in time, as they struggled to grasp it.

He thought he could see how it worked. *There* was the telescopic sight; so this must be the butt, and this the trigger . . .

He was the master now!

He gently flexed the trigger. Now he could pay them back for Postie.

'He intends to kill us, brother!'

'That is not lawful. We are prisoners . . . we are a higher species . . .' They did not sound so much afraid as outraged.

'You killed Postie!'

'He was a lower species . . .'

'See if I care . . .'

'This ape is insane.'

'Ape, if you kill us, you will make a hole in this ship. You will die too.'

'See if I care . . .' shouted Ralph again. He lined up the weapon across their heaving black bellies. Two in one shot, as Prepoc would have said . . .

'We have done nothing that merits death.' They still showed no fear; they talked to him as if he was a child in a tantrum.

'You've tortured *people*!'

'We have experimented on a lower species, looking for a cure for a killing disease. Tell me, ape – that little dog there – the one you call "Maisie" – if you took her back to your ape-earth and sold her to your crude ape-scientists – what would they do to her? They would take her into their laboratories and strap her down and cut her open and put tubes in her, and give her your worst disease and watch her die in agony. Would you kill them also, *ape?*'

Ralph could find no answer. So he pointed the blaster again, and pulled the trigger.

Instantly his whole body froze, so he couldn't even blink. Then a grey shape ghosted past him, and took the blaster from his frozen hands.

The Fefethil stared at Ralph; the centres of its eyes were as dark and cold as outer space. Beyond, the Wawaka squeaked in triumph.

'You must imprison this ape also, Fefethil. Send him to Bremis Three before he kills us all. Graft a Fefethil conscience on to *his* brain . . .'

Ralph didn't realize he could move again; till he felt the hot tears streaming down his cheeks.

*

The Fefethil ignored him; released the Wawaka from their pipe and prodded them out of sight. It was gone so long, Ralph thought he had been abandoned. Then it came back, gestured with the electric goad. Ralph followed it through the bowels of the ship; everything rusted, filthy, thick with black Wawaka-grease. The Fefethil kept hissing in disgust, but otherwise ignored him.

At last they came to a round hole, blasted in the ship's side; the edges were neat and smoothed-off, but it had smashed several pipes which dripped on the floor. Ralph guessed it was the Fefethil's work. Beyond, a golden tunnel ran upwards, spotless. They were entering the Fefethil ship. He paused, half-way through the hole.

'Postie? My friend?'

'There is nothing that can be done. He is beyond any aid, now. The quicker you come, the shorter his suffering will be. You may take the little dog.'

Ralph glanced down. Maisie had been following hopefully all this time. Ralph was ashamed he'd forgotten her. He called her to him. She whined, one paw uplifted, looking back to where Postie must still be. Ralph grabbed her and blundered up the golden tunnel, eyes blinded by fresh tears.

There was a slight whine behind; the golden tunnel was retracting. Then Ralph staggered and nearly fell; the Fefethil ship was in motion.

'Postie?' he asked again.

'Watch,' said the Fefethil icily. Ralph looked up and saw that a screen had lit up on the wall. In it, against the cold eternal stars, swam the Wawaka mirror-ship. It looked oddly beautiful, till you remembered the filth inside.

Then it disappeared.

And reappeared.

Disappeared. And reappeared; like an eye blinking faster and faster. Began to glow pink. Then red. Then blinding white. Then vanished for good.

'I have sent it into the heart of your sun,' said the Fefethil. 'Every trace of *harka* – the mould – will be burnt up. There was enough *harka* in that ship to destroy everything that lives.'

The Fefethil was silent a long time; seemed to be struggling to come to some decision. Finally it said:

'I am not one who believes that apes have no soul. If you worship some ape-god, I am willing to wait while you make requests for the possible soul of Postie.'

Ralph had never been to a funeral in his life. He tried to remember some prayers from chapel, but he couldn't even remember the Lord's Prayer straight. In the end he just mumbled, 'Please God take care of Postie' with his face buried in Maisie's fur.

'Is that all you wish to say? Then come with me. You may address me as "Theloc".'

Ralph followed him through a maze of golden tunnels, dimly lit. He kept blundering into things, and Theloc hissed softly at his clumsiness. Finally they came out into a towering grey dome, bigger than the chapel at home. The green floor yielded to his feet, like cool moss. Some sort of plastic. On the lower walls of the dome, scattered at varying heights, were long shelves covered with the same plastic. The walls of the dome were shiny, like a switched-off TV; they showed him his own face dim and distorted.

Three more Fefethil; all staring at him with that same blank Arctic coldness. The only bearable thing was Maisie. She too was shaking with fear. At least there was comfort in comforting her. Like a sick animal, he dropped to his knees and crawled under the shelter of the lowest shelf, curling himself in a ball round Maisie, thinking of nothing but stroking her gently.

But he could still hear their voices, through the plastic thing the Wawaka had put on his head. And the jeering voices of the Wawaka, somewhere far off and faint in the bowels of the ship, demanding that the ape be sent to Bremis Three as an insane murderer . . .

Then a voice said sharply:

'You must forgive the young ape, Theloc. Or he will die of loneliness.'

'Forgive, Thmeses? If he had killed the Wawaka while they were in my charge . . .'

'If this young ape dies while in your charge, we are outcasts anyway . . .'

'The ape is insane. If he had fired that *helic* and breached the hull, we would all have died . . .'

Far off, the Wawaka voices. 'The ape is insane. The ape is insane. We insist you lock him up.'

'Will you let the Wawaka be the voice of your conscience, Theloc?'

A third voice said, 'Do not do what the Wawaka want, father. What they want is never good.'

'That is untrue,' said Theloc stubbornly. 'The Wawaka have their own good.'

A fourth voice said, 'The Wawaka's good is what is good for the Wawaka.'

'Do not go against your father, Huthme.'

'I will go against my father, if my father is wrong.'

A family quarrel, however calm. It gave Ralph the courage to raise his eyes and watch. Theloc had drawn to one side, and was glaring at the others. All the furred faces were expressionless, but their ears flicked this way and that, their tails coiled and twisted. Ralph reckoned they said a lot with their tails and ears.

'The young ape is dying, Theloc!'

'Very well – you see to him, Thmeses.' He stalked off through a round door, that slid open at his approach; his tail lashed as he went. It was all very interesting in a dim, far-off way . . . but Ralph still felt the life was draining out of him, like bathwater when the plug's pulled.

'Make the young ape feel more at home, Huthme!'

The smallest, plumpest Fefethil, almost a kitten, turned to a panel in the wall and punched some buttons.

Immediately, the whole of the dome became a dark and glowing blue, like a TV screen when it's switched on. In it, a gigantic blue star exploded silently, so real that Ralph ducked for cover. When he looked again, the screen had changed to a red moonscape full of writhing worms . . . The Fefethil punched more buttons and the scene changed again, to a green glade. A rabbit hopped into the glade, so real-looking Ralph could have reached out and touched it. The dome filled with the sound of bird-song; then smells of moss and water, green shoots and flowers. The distant sound of a tractor . . .

Ralph wept for his home . . . then tensed again, as the female came and sat near him. But she only began to lick between the fingers of her hand-like paw, with a pink, velvety tongue, in a way that was somehow soothing. Her voice came, inside his head.

'My name is Thmeses, mate of Theloc. That larger Fefethil is my son, Huthmir, who flies this ship. The smaller is my daughter, Huthme, who works our weapons system. We are pleased we were able to save you. We regret your friend Postie.'

He tried to smile at her.

She flinched away, like lightning.

'Sorry,' he said, all confusion. She relaxed again.

'What does baring your teeth mean, to an ape?'

95

'That I am pleased . . .'

'With us, it means anger . . .'

'With us, it *can* mean anger . . .'

'If it means both pleasure and anger, how do apes understand each other? What does *staring* mean to apes?'

Ralph dropped his eyes guiltily. He thought of staring into Ruby's eyes. 'It means . . . love.' Then he thought of staring into Johnny Sligo's eyes, the last time they had a fight. 'And it means hate.' Then he remembered staring at the teacher at school. 'And it means you're listening to somebody.'

'So how do apes understand each other, if it means three different things?'

'And it means surprise . . . and fear . . . and nosiness.'

'No wonder apes are thought to be mad. When Fefethil show affection, they rub against each other. Do apes do such things?'

He thought of cuddling Ruby. 'With my girlfriend.'

'Girlfriend?'

He thought desperately. 'Mate?'

'Do you mate frequently?'

'We haven't mated yet.' He blushed violently.

Huthme, coming over, said, 'The ape changed colour, in his face. I didn't know apes could change colour.' She added softly, 'This ape amuses me. Can I keep him as a pet?'

'Huthme! We do not keep apes as pets.'

'Mitzah my cousin has a pet ape in his ship.'

'That is not an *intelligent* ape!'

'This ape is not *very* intelligent.'

'Be silent.' Thmeses turned again to Ralph. 'Do not be afraid of Theloc. He would not harm a hair of your body . . .'

'This ape has no hair on his body. He is bald, except the top of his head.' Huthme rolled over on her back with sheer glee, trying to catch her whipping tail between lightning-quick paws. Her tail struggled to escape; it was as if she had divided herself into two different creatures, for her own amusement. '*Wouldn't* you like to be our pet, ape? I will give you a golden collar set with sistha-stones, and all the food you want to eat!'

Thmeses silenced her, with a look that made her ears droop. Then said to Ralph, 'My mate Theloc is in two minds. He is offended by you, but he wishes to ask you favours. He does not know which way to twist his tail . . .'

96

'I will do him a favour if I can,' said Ralph, so eager to please he despised himself a bit.

'You must wait till he asks you. Meanwhile, are you hungry, ape?'

'I know what apes eat,' said Huthme. 'The charred bodies of pigs and the charred offspring of birds. The crushed and charred offspring of wheat . . .'

'No thanks,' said Ralph hurriedly. 'I'm not really hungry.'.

CHAPTER 14

'Come with me, ape!'

Alone with Theloc, Ralph's unease returned. The control-cabin was full of the smell of him. Not a foul, greasy smell, like the Wawaka, but a dusty, peppery smell, so that Ralph constantly felt about to sneeze. The Fefethil's breathing was quicker and shallower than his own; his nostrils flared as he breathed, and the leathery patch on the end of his nose was damp. His breath was cool on Ralph's cheek; cooler than Ruby's.

Theloc was taller than him; but his chest was so narrow that Ralph could almost have put his hands round it. Theloc's body and neck swivelled so much he looked almost as supple as a snake. And patches of his fur were given to fits of trembling. Theloc would break off speaking to beat them into flat sleekness with an enormously long purplish tongue. It was as if his calmness of mind was paid for by these tiny constant rebellions in his fur, that had to be suppressed by the tongue . . . Sometimes long, grey claws emerged from Theloc's stubby, furry fingertips. He could tear off my face with one slap, thought Ralph. The small, dainty teeth, only visible when he licked himself, were equally sharp. A creature of spears hidden in fur . . .

The eyes were scariest of all. Reduced to thin slits, they made the whole face into an expressionless, furry helmet; but when the pupils grew large and round, they looked almost human, yet infinitely sad.

So Theloc stood, his face unreadable. But his tail moved up in a slow painful curve, till it found rest by curling round a convenient pipe. Ralph thought the Fefethil embarrassed . . .

'Ape, I forgive you.'

Ralph said 'Thank you' equally solemnly. Then added, 'Sorry – I was so angry!'

'Are not young apes taught to control their rage? Still, no matter, I forgive you.'

'Thank you,' said Ralph solemnly again. He wondered if he was going to stand there all day, saying thank you solemnly to Theloc.

'Ape, you have the right to be returned instantly to the time and place from which the Wawaka stole you. You also have the right to have your memory washed clean of all that has happened. I will return you shortly . . . but I would rather you remembered all that has happened . . .'

'OK,' said Ralph. 'I'd rather know what was killing me . . .' But he shivered at the memories.

The Fefethil seemed to read his thoughts.

'The Wawaka are not the worst race in the universe. They do not harm any of their own kind. That much they have learnt. They are attached to the little dog, Maisie. They have cured all her diseases and are anxious for her welfare. They would like to take her into captivity with them. I hope you will consent – they have not much to hope for now, where they are going . . .'

'If they aren't the worst race in the universe, I'd like to know what is . . .'

The Fefethil was silent a long time. 'Do you really wish to know?'

'I wouldn't have asked if I hadn't,' said Ralph. But he trembled.

The Fefethil stared out of the window, at the earth spinning past. 'The apes are the worst. Apes kill other apes. They are the only intelligent race left that kill their own kind. Apes poison the air other apes breathe; they let other apes starve to death. Apes experiment on other apes. Apes have killed their own children, their mates, their mothers . . . It is lucky apes are so primitive, or they would have killed everything in the universe by now.'

'We aren't all *that* primitive. We've been to the moon. We've got atomic energy . . .'

'There are many who hope you will poison yourselves with it, before you learn enough to trouble the universe . . .'

'Who are these . . . many?'

'You must realize, ape, when Lord Merethon made the universe, he made all living worlds the same. Each contained apes, cats, dogs, fish . . . But on each world, a different species prospered. In your world, the apes. In mine, the cats. Each learnt to walk upright, to grasp tools, to think. Except there are other ways to prosper besides walking and grasping . . . the highest race in the universe, Merethon's Children, would look to you like a pool of slime. Yet they could freeze you to a block of ice, by thought alone, before you came within a million miles of their planet. But don't worry – they still have hope for the apes. But for them, your world would have been

99

an empty shell, robbed of its gold and iron and plutonium, before the first ape walked upright . . .'

'Is that what Prepoc was doing . . . protecting us . . . when he got killed?'

'Your beloved Prepoc, who has caused all this trouble? No, Prepoc was not a peaceful guardian like me. Prepoc was a savage, who lived to hunt and kill. But for Prepoc and his love of hunting, we should not be in the trouble we are now.'

Theloc sounded so desperate that fear squeezed Ralph's belly. '*What* trouble? You can cope with the Wawaka – you always do!'

The Fefethil's tail sagged; its ears drooped slightly. 'Two millennia ago, ape, when your land was all trees and ruled by the red-helmets, our universe was invaded by a race we called the Attock. We do not know where they came from, but they settled on the planet Brunitaj. We never found out what happened to the bears who had lived on Brunitaj . . . But the Attock rejoiced in evil; in death to all other creatures. It was they who brought the mould disease, harka, for which the Wawaka have still found no cure, though it invades the wombs of their females, and kills half their young before they are born and kills them all in the end . . . It was the Attock who tore up the singing trees of Apulca, who did nothing in their lives save give pleasure to others . . .

'Our worlds had been at peace for many centuries. Few knew how to fight; few could bear to kill. The Wawaka, yes. But they were very primitive then. Only the Fefethil still killed – for food. And had the brain to beat the Attock. We had Prepoc, war-leader. And Sephotic, who was no warrior, but who could devise machines and horrors that would kill the Attock. Sephotic invented things that could destroy whole planets. That is why he was called Sephotic World-eater . . .

'Every race worked to make the machines of Sephotic; even Merethon's Children. He built the ships; Prepoc led them. In seven great battles we destroyed the Attock. In the end, we destroyed Brunitaj. They say it cracked open like an egg . . .

'But the three kings of the Attock escaped the ruin of Brunitaj. We pursued them through space and crippled their ship. It fell to earth in your world. We sealed off your world. We could have lifted the Attock from it at our ease, as you might lift a specimen from a jar . . . it was over.

'But Sephotic desired to be a great hunter, like Prepoc. With Prepoc and a few friends, he would descend to your world and hunt the Attock on foot, for sport . . .

'Something went wrong – we never knew what. Sephotic was always clumsy, for a Fefethil; they said his brain stood in the way of his paws. And Prepoc was tired, and those with him. The Attock had few weapons left, except the fury of their despair . . . but all died. The Attock, Sephotic, Prepoc and his friends. It is said that Prepoc hunted down the Attock alone, after all his friends were dead. And killed all three with one blaster-shot.

'There was great grief for the death of Prepoc; and for the death of Sephotic. They were buried where they fell; on your world. Prepoc in a humble tomb, with his weapons around him, like a simple hunter. For he was humble in everything, except his hunting. Sephotic in a great tomb, full of the strange and terrible weapons he had made. Then the tombs were sealed, and the minds of those who had made them were emptied, so that it was forgotten even where those tombs were. Except that Prepoc stands guard still, over the tomb of his friend, Sephotic.

'And such was the horror of the machines that destroyed the Attock that when the rest had returned to my world, they were all destroyed, and Sephotic's plans and designs with them. And the minds of all who had helped to make them were also wiped clean of memories. Merethon's Children saw to that. For they said that if those plans were left existing, there would come a time when some race would discover and use them . . . to destroy and enslave all.

'That time has come, ape. Always the Wawaka were aggressive; but they were crude and clumsy fools. Then halenium was discovered on their planet, a metal so lovely that all the races were driven mad for it and the pleasure it gave. The Wawaka sold it to them, and gained wealth beyond dreams. And they used that wealth to build ships to trouble the worlds with. They dream of conquest . . . greatness . . . destiny.'

'Like . . . Hitler?'

'And other apes, who have been even madder than the rest . . .'

'So that's why the Wawaka are here?'

'Yes, they sent their poor stupid dog-philosophers to the libraries of the Children of Merethon, saying they sought knowledge to write a history of their race. Merethon's Children knew they were looking for the tomb of Sephotic. But they also knew the tomb was concealed for ever by the devices of Sephotic. The Wawaka hung around the fringes of your world, and sometimes broke the law and landed, but we simply came and took them away again . . . though they gave some poor apes a great fright.'

101

'Werewolves?'

'Yes – always the stupid Wawaka hung around your graveyards, looking for the tomb of Sephotic. It was all laughable . . . till *you* found the tomb of Prepoc. Now, we watch, night and day, the Wawaka who watch your earth. We know when they break the law by entering your atmosphere. We block their radio-transmissions instantly. But parts of messages get through. We do not know how much the lords of the Wawaka know. We will take *these* Wawaka away, but more will come. I do not think any Wawaka now left free know who you are, but they know where you live, and they know you have found the tomb of Prepoc.

'If you do not open the tomb of Prepoc again, you will be safe. Radiations come from the tomb of Prepoc like no others in your world. It comes from everything left of him, and it clings to anyone who handles it. And they can pick it up, far out in space. That is why they took Postie, and the mailbags from the post-office.'

'And that's why they took the sewage-station. They took my bathwater, and the water from Mam's washing-machine . . .'

'You are no fool, for an ape.'

'Me? I'm dead thick. I've only got two O levels.'

'You have a sympathy with other animals, other races, your ape-scientists will never have. That is why I am tempted to ask you . . .'

'What?'

'To try to find the tomb of Sephotic.'

'What, *me*?'

'We are not even allowed to search for it. We may only enter your atmosphere to remove Wawaka. Anything else is forbidden, by our harshest law. It would be the sin of *nithila* – world-breaking.'

'But why *me*? If I got in touch with some scientists . . .'

'Ape, who knows these fells like you? Who knows the lead-mines, every hidden place? Who knows the ways of the animals who live there? If any ape finds the tomb of Sephotic, it will be you. You found the tomb of Prepoc.'

'But scientists have . . .'

'Your ape-scientists are scoffers, and therefore blind. There is only you, ape. It is not likely you will find Sephotic; but no other ape will.'

'And if I do . . . how do I tell you?'

The Fefethil's tail twisted in pure agony. 'I cannot give you the means of summoning me. That alone would be the sin of *nithila*. It would begin to twist you, to change the history of your world. All I

102

may say is, if you do something that brings the Wawaka to your world again, we shall not be far behind.'

'Well,' said Ralph, 'maybe if I found Sephotic, you'd think better of us apes . . .'

'Ape, you are an ape beyond price.'

'Maybe if I found Sephotic, you'd start calling us "men" instead.'

'Ape, if you find Sephotic, I will call you "man". But come, I have two gifts I *may* give you.'

Theloc opened a cupboard that was horrifyingly like the cupboards of the Wawaka; except it was golden, spotlessly clean and contained a golden seat. The Fefethil noticed Ralph's fear, and went and sat inside the cupboard himself. Immediately, a mass of golden tentacles descended on him, thrusting pads across his eyes, thrusting tendrils up his nose and ears and mouth. One golden arm, bearing tiny scissors, snipped off a tuft of his grey fur and dropped it into a glass cylinder, where it was first whirled to a grey mush, and then burnt in a long flame. It was like watching Theloc being eaten alive by a golden octopus. But, in what seemed less than a minute, Theloc emerged unharmed, just smoothing down the fur of his chest where the tiny snippet had been removed.

The cupboard spoke through the plastic device on Ralph's head. It sounded exactly like another Fefethil, only even calmer.

'Why have you tested yourself, Theloc? You were only tested two days ago, and your health is perfect. Are you anxious?'

'It was to reassure the ape . . .'

'Put in the ape now. I have the norms for apes.'

And in Ralph went; into the pit of golden snakes. It felt abominable; he felt like screaming; only his mouth and throat were full of golden tentacles, which made him retch. It seemed to go on far longer than it had for Theloc . . . Then quite suddenly he was free to leap out and stand shaking. But worse followed. The cupboard spoke.

'The young ape is seriously ill. He is not yet mature but his teeth are rotting and his fur losing colour. He has been poisoned by large doses of sucrose, aluminium and lead. He is deficient in many trace elements, especially the metal selenium. He shows radioactive traces he should not have at all . . .'

'Is he dying?' Theloc's tail lashed with anxiety.

'He is not yet dying, but he is living in great misery – there are

103

already arthritic deposits in his joints. He must be treated immediately . . .'

'Will you be in time?'

'He is still young – the damage is not irreversible. *Who* has been
poisoning this ape?'

'The apes poison themselves . . .'

'I find no trace of mental aberration. He is slow and ill-taught, but
quite sane.'

Theloc turned to Ralph. 'It is your right to refuse treatment . . .'

'No,' said Ralph. 'I'd better be done . . .' The mention of arthritis
had terrified him; he remembered his Dad's. Stoically, he climbed
back on to the golden seat.

'The machine will render you unconscious,' warned Theloc. 'All
your blood must be taken from you and cleansed . . .'

'Hey!' shouted Ralph. Too late. The golden seat had pricked him in
his bottom, and he knew nothing else.

There was a soft paw, patting his nose.

'Wake up, ape! Are you going to hibernate, like the bears?'

He grabbed for the paw, and caught it, amazed by the speed of his
own hand. So was the paw; it struggled and flexed its claws, frantic
to escape. But his hand was too strong for it; he was amazed by the
strength of his own hand.

'Ape, you are hurting me,' said Huthme.

'Serves you right,' said Thmeses. 'You tormented the ape while he
was ill.'

Ralph opened his eyes and looked at them all. Quite calmly for the
first time. He accepted them; they were Fefethil; neither talking cats,
nor men in furry disguises, but simply Fefethil. Who had as much
right to exist as he did. He saw them with great clarity; the
slightest of furrows on Theloc's brow; the tiny flick of anxiety in
Thmeses' tail. He let go Huthme's paw, and said, teasing 'Sorry, little
sister!'

He swung off the seat with one smooth movement. All his aches
and pains were gone. His body moved as if it had been oiled. He felt
new. A king among kings.

There was a pipe running across the ceiling of the medical room.
He leapt for it, and to his surprise managed to grasp it, and haul
himself up to sit astride.

Then he looked down. They were all staring up at him.

'The ape has recovered his apehood,' said Huthme.

'You must go,' said Theloc. 'You have been gone six hours; we cannot stretch time too far.'

'You will be there when I need you?'

'Where else would we be?'

'Don't you ever go home?'

'We have no home. Our planet was destroyed when they destroyed the machines that slew the Attock. There was no other way. It makes us safer guardians; we have the power, but we are scattered across space. We only meet to mate our young. Only we remember our world with two red suns . : .'

Ralph had never heard such quiet sadness. 'What will happen to you, then? In the end?'

'We shall die in space. Our last voyage will be into the heart of some sun. We buried Prepoc on your little wet planet, and look at the evil that has come from that. Huthme and Huthmir will mate, and have ships of their own. *Our* names will be remembered once a year, in the great hall of the Children of Merethon . . .'

'I'm sorry.'

'Do not pity us. Fire is a clean death. Would you rather die of the mould, as the Wawaka do? . . . Here is your other gift – the one I am allowed to give you, for it may undo harm already done.' Theloc handed Ralph a small, shiny, soft package. Silvery.

'What is it?'

'A radiation-bag. It will block all the radiations that Prepoc's equipment gives off, that the Wawaka can detect. It may be of no use to you at all – but it is also unbreakable and waterproof.'

And suddenly, Ralph was running down the hillside again, into Unthank in the peaceful sunset. Mam was still taking her knickers off the washing-line. Ruby was waving. And his jeans and boots were whole again; just battered.

CHAPTER 15

Ralph straightened up, eased his back, wiped his brow. The last three days, Jack Norton had had the combine-harvester in, to cut his wheat. Three days of endlessly lifting bales of straw on to a trailer pulled by a tractor. Jack's youngest, Harry, ten years old, drove the tractor. Ten-year-olds driving tractors was illegal; fat lot Jack Norton cared about that. He wasn't going to waste a grown man driving a tractor. Grown men were used, like Ralph and Billy, Jack's eldest, to heave bloody great bales of straw on to the trailer. Till their backs broke.

Ralph hated the combine. It went inhumanly quick. It did not tire, like men did, as the day went on. It made straw-bales inhumanly large, so that one man couldn't lift them. Every time Ralph and Billy linked arms to lift one, Ralph felt the muscles at the base of his stomach strain. He was terrified of getting a rupture . . . too many farmhands ended up with ruptures . . .

'Tea up,' shouted Jack jovially, coming through the gate carrying a large basket. Ralph was glad Jack's back could take the strain of *that*. Still, there'd be beer-bottles full of cold, sweet tea without milk. Nothing like cold tea when you're sweating. Didn't make you dopey, like beer, that Billy was far too fond of in the middle of the day . . .

And Mrs Norton, at least, was generous. Great wedges of juicy apple-pie. Luckily, Billy didn't like it, and gave Ralph his share, with fingers blackened by the dark-brown grime off the straw.

Ralph settled, with his two pieces, in the shade under the trailer; closed his eyes and bit into the first piece. Nearly as good as kissing Ruby. Then he half-dozed, listening to Jack's querulous voice talking to Billy's deep rumble, as distant and abstract as music on a fading tranny.

In spite of the combine, it had been a good week. Sun, sweat, the endless shower of golden grain into the hopper. It burnt away dark memories into dark dreams . . .

Nothing frightening had happened. The air had failed to fall apart.

Nothing need ever happen again, if he had the sense to keep away from Prepoc.

'Hey up,' he heard Jack yelp suddenly. 'T'fell's on fire! Look, up yonder by't cairn!'

'Ga wey,' said Billy, sleepily. 'You're getting dafter, our dad. Fell's too wet – bin too much rain this year.'

'Look, I telt thee, clouds of smoke. Just round top of't cairn.' They were all on their feet now, shading their eyes against the intense pale glare of the blue sky.

'Flock o' birds,' said Billy in disgust, and sat down against the tractor wheel again. 'Finches always start flockin' this time o' year. Look down't field.' He pointed to where a mixed flock of sparrows and finches were busy with multi-fluttering wings among the grain spilled from the combine.

'An' what is there for finches to eat, up on't fell?' demanded Jack. 'Tell me that, then!'

'Sheep-shit,' said Billy, and tipped his cap over his eyes for a post-lunch snooze. 'Never short o' sheep-shit on't fell.'

'Finches don't eat sheep-shit.' Jack, not being tired from doing any amount of work, was displaying an irritating amount of energy. 'I'll go an' get granda's spy-glass, that's what I'll do. Bet you a quid it's heather smouldering, our Billy.'

'You're on,' said Billy, not bothering to remove his cap from his eyes. Jack swished off through the stubble in a rage; Ralph heard his car start. Ralph went on looking up the fell; there was definitely a cloud of *something* dark swirling in the air above the far-distant cairn: something that came and went like smoke; but it moved this way and that, though the air was hot and still; and it had none of the density of a big fire's smoke.

In an amazingly short time, Jack's car was back. He strode up the stubble triumphantly, pulling out to its full length an old brass telescope, dull green with disuse. He poked his thumb into the eyepiece to clear out the dust. 'Now we'll see. Me granda was a captain . . .'

'He was a Chief Petty Officer,' said Billy. 'An' he was chucked out o't navy for drink an' getting a mate's wife pregnant. Even in't middle of't Fust World War, they could do wi'out Grandad.'

But Jack had put the telescope to his eye; swaying slightly as a combination of booze, the noonday heat and the telescope's magnification made him dizzy.

'Damn me,' he said bitterly. 'Birds it is. A gurt flock of crows. Never seen so many crows.'

107

'A dead sheep,' said Billy, holding out an expectant hand, still without taking his cap from over his eyes. 'That's a quid you owe me, our dad.'

'I'll give it you later,' said Jack. 'Haven't got any money on me.'

'He never has, when it comes to payin' debts.' Billy was too drowsy to be bitter.

But Jack would not let the matter rest. 'Never *seen* so many crows. Must be every crow in Cumberland.'

'At least twenty,' said Billy dreamily. 'It'll still cost yer a pound.'

'Look, Ralph, look!' Jack thrust the telescope into Ralph's hands. Ralph took out his handkerchief, and carefully cleaned the thumb-printed lenses. His heart was hammering in his chest. He heard Jack say, 'That's more than any dead sheep fetching them . . .'

'All right,' said Billy, 'a dead hoss, then.'

'Who's hoss? Ain't no hosses on our fell.'

Ralph raised the telescope. It waved about wildly all over the sky, because his hands were shaking so. A glimpse of stone wall jumped into the pale blue circle, then jumped out again. He got it again, managed to hold it till he got it into focus. It was certainly a very good telescope; terrific magnification. A flock of sheep, lower down the fell, looked so close and detailed he could have sent the dogs after them.

He searched along the horizon, till he came to the cairn.

He knew at once its outline was altered; stones had fallen off. But you could hardly see any stones, because the cairn was thick with crows, hopping frantically, quarrelling over something invisible behind the cairn; quarrelling about bits of stuff they held in their beaks . . . The crows had certainly found some dead thing and were tearing it apart. And it must be bigger than a sheep, like Jack said. You never got more than twenty crows round a dead sheep at once, and here the air was full of them, and more coming all the time. It must be absolute pandemonium up there, the cawing and squawking and shrieking. But all silent through the telescope, like an old movie . . .

Ruby said she'd closed the coffin; piled back the stones as best she could. She mustn't have closed the coffin properly. It must have sprung open like an overfull suitcase, sending the stones scattering . . . exposing Prepoc's body.

Then he remembered the coffin lid didn't spring open; you had to use quite a lot of strength to lift it. Somebody had pulled the stones off and opened the coffin, and left it open . . . kids?

But he knew he was fooling himself. No local kid would ever toil up the fell in this heat. And fell-walkers, if they'd found Prepoc, would have closed the coffin and gone for the police.

He knew who'd done it.

Wawaka.

And he knew why. Because they hoped he'd notice, and go hurrying up to see what was wrong with Prepoc. They didn't know who he was, but they knew he'd keep looking at the cairn; would notice sooner or later. And when he went up, all worried and unsuspecting, they'd *have* him ...

As if Jack Norton could read his thoughts, he said:

'Better take a walk up there, Ralph. Could be a whole flock, poisoned theirselves wi' eatin' something. Or mebbe some walker-feller broke his neck ...'

'*Now*, Mr Norton?' Ralph was shaking all over. But Jack was far too busy to notice, kicking Billy back into wakefulness with a thoughtful toe.

'Naw,' said Jack. 'Tomorrow'll do. Whatever's up there is dead by now. We've got this field to clear. Can't have you laikin' up't fell when there's work to be done.' At the very mention of work he yawned and said, 'Got ter see a man in Gamblesby.' He turned towards his car, picking up the telescope.

'Can I borrow the spyglass, Mr Norton,' said Ralph suddenly. 'Keep an eye on things till I can get up there?'

Jack's fingers relaxed from round it. 'Tek care you don't drop it; it's a family heirloom, that.'

'Where we goin' with the telescope, Ralph?' asked Ruby. 'Bird-watching?' She was wearing the wrong sort of shoes again, and stumbling along desperately some yards behind.

'Low End,' said Ralph. He felt a beast, walking so fast. But he was *worried*.

'What's the rush? Old birds won't fly away!'

'Something I want to see. C'mon! Why don't you take your shoes off? Grass is soft enough ...' She took her shoes off. Her feet were much prettier than her shoes; long and slim with longish toes. He made himself walk behind her, so he wouldn't be tempted to leave her behind again; watched her as she walked ahead; the slim muscles of her legs. But he didn't feel like *that* this evening. Too tense.

109

Low End was a detached bit of the fell, standing a little way off in the Eden Valley. A conical hill, covered in trees; part of the civilized lowland; part of Mason's Farm, cut off from the fell by the Alston road climbing Hartside Height, which always had a stream of cars on it, even this time of night. That's why he'd judged it safe to bring Ruby. The Wawaka wouldn't dare show themselves on the open road . . .

It was shady, under the big trees; the grass was long, green and soft. Ruby kept glancing at it meaningfully. She must be feeling romantic again. Hard luck!

At the top was a tiny clearing, looking towards the fell, containing just one great horse-chestnut. They were much nearer the cairn here; the clustering clouds of birds were clear in view.

'Oh, Ralph, what's happening now?' Ruby looked at him fearfully, eyes wide, the colour draining from her cheeks, leaving her carefully applied lipstick looking like fat, pink graffiti.

'That's what I'm going to find out.' He'd hung the telescope round his body on a lanyard cut from Mam's second-best washing-line. Now he jumped for the lowest branch of the horse-chestnut. He looked down on her, overwhelmingly glad she was there. 'Keep down. Outa sight. Have a fag!'

He threw down his fag-tin, then a box of matches. She slunk obediently down behind the tree-trunk, and he climbed, cheerfully accompanied by the smell of her Silk Cut. The horse-chestnut was easy to climb; the branches were almost like a spiral staircase. Soon he was within five feet of the top. A good strong tree; didn't even sway. He got his bottom to a fork in the branches, and tied himself in place with more washing-line. Then he extended the telescope, quite unafraid of falling. Theloc's medical-machine *had* made him into a better ape, he thought grimly.

The first thing he noticed was the sheep. This time of night, in sunny weather, they should be lying down chewing the cud, in little groups all over the face of the fell. Instead, they were pressed against the bottom fence in a desperate huddle, all on their feet and not even snatching a tuft of grass. Terrified out of their wits by something higher up the fell.

And he could tell the exact position of what they were scared of, even if it was invisible. For most of the fellside was open, from this angle. But, some distance below the cairn, there was a long, horizontal, outcrop of rock, and a row of mounds; the overgrown spoilheaps of the old lead-mines.

So they were lying in wait there; for the first silly person who walked up to see what was going on round the cairn. They'd catch him while he was still slogging uphill, panting, with his head down, at his least alert . . .

Clever, the Wawaka. But not clever enough for an ape who happened to be a shepherd.

He swept the telescope along the spoilheaps. Not a trace of movement. Except the rabbits that normally fed there at dusk were much lower down tonight. And twice he saw lapwings make for the spoilheaps to roost, then swerve away at the last moment . . .

So the Wawaka were occupying the whole line of spoilheaps, covering a front of two hundred yards. How many? Four? Six? That was the next thing to find out. He mightn't be over-bright, but as a shepherd he had plenty of patience.

Looking up the tree twenty minutes later, Ruby saw him still sitting as still as a stone. So still, she was impelled to call 'You all right?'

'Yeh!' He had just located a fourth pair of black ears, as they rose cautiously in turn above the spoilheaps. Four, then.

It gave him a sense of power over them. He could see them; but they couldn't see him. He muttered to himself: 'Now I got you, me beauties,' as if they were sheep; or foxes.

His mood was changing; less scared, more angry. If *he* didn't go up tomorrow, sooner or later somebody else would. Some poor shepherd or policeman, or even some curious kid. And they'd have no chance; they'd end up in one of those obscene cupboards, with the harka-mould spreading slowly over them. Innocent; as Postie had been innocent . . .

The Wawaka were in *his* world; preying on *his* people. Like crows when they pecked the eyes out of newborn lambs. Vermin. He must kill them, because they were vermin.

But how? Even with Prepoc's helmet and blaster, they were four against one. They'd see him coming . . . miles off.

He studied the face of his beloved fell, harder than he'd ever studied it in his life.

Just below the cairn was a swamp or sink-hole. Full of black slime and moss. Oozing water into five black streams or burns that ran down the face of the fell. Four of the black burns ran down through the spoilheaps, slowly spreading further apart, like the fingers of a hand. The fifth, like a thumb of that hand, wandered away by itself,

111

much further to the right. It was wider and deeper, more full of water than the others, and ran under the Alston road in a wide culvert.

If he went up through that culvert, and walked up the bed of the burn, he'd be below ground level nearly all the way. The noise of the running water would drown any noise he made. He could get behind them, attack from an angle they would never expect.

But suppose they smelled him? Like dogs, they'd have a terrific sense of smell . . . He held up a finger to test the wind. It was blowing from the left. It would blow from them to him, as he went up the burn; they would smell nothing. And it was a gentle little wind, that would blow steadily all night. Unless the weather got worse . . . He looked at the sky; not a cloud in sight. The weather would not change.

And if he carried Prepoc's helmet and blaster and the red egg in the radiation-proof bag Theloc had given him, they wouldn't pick up any radiation either.

Then he had an even better idea. If, once he was behind the Wawaka, he took little balls of paste from the red egg and threw them into the burns, the radiation would rush down on the Wawaka, with the speed of the water, and panic them . . .

He saw it all now. The Wawaka in the dark, jumpy, nervy. The radiation in the burns coming at them from behind. The Wawaka trying to attack uphill, over the bumpy, slippery, unfamiliar tussocks. Prepoc's helmet showing them up clearly . . . Prepoc would be disappointed to find only four Wawaka . . . hardly a fight at all to him. Wawaka slipping, sliding, panicking . . . oh, most enjoyable. Four in one shot? A red fighting glee filled Ralph's mind . . .

Then the cold thought struck him. He must go tonight. After Mam had gone to bed. His fear came back, and he began to shake.

But he had made up his mind; they were vermin, and he would rid his world of them. If he didn't go tonight, he would have to go tomorrow, when he would stand no chance at all. He untied himself and came down the tree so fast he nearly fell.

Ruby got up, all pale. 'Some of them crows is dying,' she said. 'They're lying on the ground not moving, and other crows is eating them and dying as well.'

He trained the telescope on the cairn itself for the first time. Around its broken sides was a black shining carpet of dead crows. They must be eating Prepoc's embalmed body, and being poisoned by it. A black stain of death, spreading out from the cairn . . .

He hated crows. But they were still earth-crows, so he hated the Wawaka even more. He would think of the dying crows tonight, as he climbed the burn, to give himself strength.

'Good riddance to bad rubbish,' he said to Ruby.

She thought he meant the crows; but he didn't.

CHAPTER 16

Mam came in to say goodnight about ten, as usual. She went to bed early to save the electric bill. And as usual, she picked up the clothes he'd tossed down, and beat them into neat folded shapes with her work-reddened hands. Usually, he hated her doing this; but tonight she might be doing it for the last time . . .

She caught him watching. 'What's got you so pussy-struck? You look like a man who's going to be hanged in the morning. You *sure* you haven't got Ruby in the family way?'

'We don't do that sort of thing!'

'You must be the last young couple in England that doesn't. Still, you were always slow, our Ralph.'

'Look – would you rather we did or we didn't?' He was suddenly irritated beyond belief with her. Anyway, it got rid of her. She just said 'Pah' and bustled out. Then he was sorry; if he wasn't lucky tonight, he'd seen the last of her for ever. She was just through the wall in her own bedroom, but she might as well be a thousand miles away. He suddenly felt like crying. Instead, he drew what comfort he could from the sounds of her settling for the night. Clink of water-ewer on bowl; the violent sounds of spitting as she cleaned her teeth. Then the springs creaking in the great cold bed she'd once shared with his father. Did she still miss his father, after eight years? Would she miss *him*, if he didn't come back?

At half-past ten he switched his light off, and lay in the dark, eyes open. Mam always listened for the click of his switch, and if it was too long coming, she hammered on the wall . . . He was so *tired*; it would have been so easy to roll over and go to sleep. But then the morning would leap on him like a tiger . . . He kept himself awake by listening to the sounds of the village going to sleep. The clink of milk-bottles; Jack Norton, misjudging the corner through drink, sending one of the empty milk-churns that lived by his gate rolling over and over down the cobbled lane. Then there was just the sound of sheep cropping grass in the lower field, and Mam having her usual late-night fight with the bedsprings. Finally, even she was silent; nothing would wake her till morning . . .

Time to go. How many sweaters? It was cold on the fell at night, even in the middle of summer. He lingered over his best pale-blue sweater; he couldn't bear the thought of mould growing over it . . . should he leave it behind, safe, to wait for him? Then he thought, to hell with it, and put it on anyway.

His fags? Fags and matches stood ready, in his waterproof tin. But he'd be tempted to have a drag, and the smell would give him away. But he'd take them just the same. Maybe he'd get to smoke a victory-fag, like soldiers on the telly . . .

Finally, he crept out of the house, leaving the front door unlocked. If he lost his nerve and came back early, he didn't want to have to knock Mam up and have her asking questions . . .

As he passed the farm-gate, Jet and Nance roused in their kennel, and came out to meet him, stretching and rattling their chains, ready for a romp. At harvest-time they were underworked and bored all day. Should he take them?

As far as they'd dare go. They'd be company. They had better ears and noses; he felt naked on the fell without them. And the Wawaka wouldn't harm *them*. Probably cure all their diseases, like they had with Maisie . . .

Postie . . . at the memory, terror left him limp and shaking, so he had to hold on to the gatepost. Then he thought he only had to get to the first lead-mine, and he'd have the helmet, and Prepoc would be with him too.

He wrapped the helmet and blaster and egg in the radiation-bag, and slung it on his back with a bit of clothes-line. The helmet bumped against the blaster as he walked. It made less noise than his footsteps; but it still irritated him. He felt his head was going to burst; every nerve in his body seemed to have a life of its own; he had a solid lump of wind in his gut that he couldn't seem to belch away. But he went on; he knew he was safe as far as the culvert, because he could still see the headlights of late lorries and cars ahead and above, as they climbed Hartside Height. Suddenly, he felt like a soldier, yomping to Port Stanley. He wondered if they'd felt as lonely as this, yomping to Port Stanley . . .

He slipped into the culvert; the water of the burn ran swiftly and shallowly over his boots, making his feet cold without making them wet; Mam always kept his boots well-dubbined.

115

The arched roof of the culvert vibrated; only a little when a car went over it, but quite alarmingly for a juggernaut . . .

Beyond the culvert, the walls of the burn were already above his head; he felt a little safer; the sound of the burn hid the splashes he made as he slipped and slithered up the bed of slimy stones. Thank God the walls of the burn were too high for the collies to jump out of now . . . but they seemed quite happy sniffing around the wet stones.

Then, as they went higher, they grew uneasy; stopping to raise their heads and scent the air with deep breaths. They closed in towards him for protection . . . so the Wawaka were still there. There *was* going to be a battle tonight. Quite soon if they'd set a Wawaka to guard *this* burn . . .

But they hadn't. After what seemed an eternity of climbing up through water, the collies stopped looking ahead nervously, and started looking over their shoulders instead. He was past the spoil-heaps. The collies quickened their pace, moving away from trouble . . . Ralph knew he was going to reach the cairn.

The burn grew shallower as it neared its source in the sink-hole. He had to walk crouched to stay under cover. When the burn got too narrow to walk in, he took to the heather and crawled.

Then, without warning, dead crows were scrunching under his feet and hands; he nearly screamed as he crawled through the sea of cold feathers and bone. But he'd reached the crest; there was the broken cairn looming against the night sky. He crouched at the base of it. He'd done it!

The first bit, anyway. With stiff, cold and trembling fingers, he opened the radiation-bag and crawled inside with the helmet and blaster. The bag extended to take him; it was nearly as big as a two-man tent. He put on the helmet and pulled down the visor . . . felt the little tentacles crawl into his mouth and ears . . . then looked up.

The bag seemed to be transparent. What was more, a dim green light seemed to be shining over the whole fell. Ralph thought at first the moon had come out, and cowered down lest he be seen. Then he realized the green light was simply a function of the helmet; for night-fighting. Like those image-intensifiers the army used, that Argie Button talked about so much. Only, much better than any army image-intensifier, the helmet showed up the enemy, glowing red against the green; selected targets. Not four Wawaka, but six, lying down the slope with their backs to him, utterly unaware of his presence. And somehow he knew that if they did become aware of him, their red images would suddenly glow brighter, to orange, as the helmet warned him. Ralph noticed wryly that one of the Wawaka was very close to the burn he'd come up. A sentry after all; but a sentry half-asleep.

Typical Wawaka, sneered Prepoc, coming into his head and into the driving-seat with a rush, as the helmet microchips fed data into Ralph's brain. Prepoc established, with much disappointment, that the foe was simply six more worthless Wawaka, and that again they deserved to die for the cardinal sin of *nithila*, world-breaking . . .

Prepoc was so utterly calm; as if the Wawaka were only images in a funfair space-wars machine. He took his time looking round, and noticed something that Ralph would have missed.

Just beyond the cairn, hidden from the valley by the bowl of the fell, was the Wawaka's mirror-ship. The helmet told him that the ship was unmanned, empty, awaiting its cargo of earth-captives. Around it lay the glitter of its defensive force-field, which was proof against Prepoc's old blaster. The ship was not resting on the uneven surface of the fell, but floating on its force-field about three feet above it.

Coolly, Prepoc made his preparations. Ralph's fingers formed four tiny pellets of the green paste; tiny because it might be a long battle, and the paste was not to be wasted. Then Prepoc called the trembling collies into the radiation-bag with him; soothing them with Ralph's voice, Ralph's gentle hands. The collies trembled like running motors, under Ralph's hands. Then Prepoc smeared a small amount of the green paste on each of their necks, rubbing it well into the black hair.

Then he burst open the bag, shouting in Ralph's voice, 'Ga wey, Nance; ga wey, Jet!'

The collies instinct to herd was stronger than their fear of the Wawaka.

Instinctively, they streaked off down the fellside in huge half-circles, one to the left and one to the right of the Wawaka. Prepoc gauged the progress of their run, then crawled swiftly to each of the four burns, dropping a pellet in each. Watched through his visor as the pellets began to melt in the running water, making the streams radioactive. Now the burns were rushing down their new radiation towards the Wakawa . . . spreading like glowing veins, a web of radioactivity round the Wawaka's feet.

The effect on the Wawaka was chaotic. They spotted the collies first, coming from a totally unexpected direction, with the radio-activity of the Fefethil upon them. So they were enemy . . . but they

117

were also recognized as dogs. And to the Wawaka, dog did not eat dog . . . they were paralysed by confusion. By the time they finally opened fire, the dogs were already fleeing towards the valley and home, an impossible moving target as they streaked across the humpy, broken ground.

Then suddenly the Fefethil radiation in the burns was all around their feet, and the minds of the Wawaka collapsed in chaos. They fired wildly in every direction. Ralph saw one of them explode in a blaze of radiation, as the blaster-beam of another hit it. Ralph saw another Wawaka blast off its own feet.

But Prepoc turned his back on them, and aimed towards the mirror-ship, still resting on its force-field on the sweet-smelling heather. He did not aim at the ship direct; he fired at the fellside upon which the right-hand half of the ship rested. The blaster scooped out a great trench beneath it. The mirror-ship began to tip, as its support vanished. It tipped on to its edge, then slowly, slowly over on to its back, like some great ocean-liner sinking, its portholes all ablaze; like the *Titanic* in the movie . . .

The mirror-ship was designed for many things. It could travel in space and, if need be, time. It could spin and turn in its own length. But it was not designed to lie upside down, with its own force-field as well as earth-gravity grinding it into the ground and tearing at its innards.

Ralph heard something break loose inside, and crash down on to something else. There was a tinkle like breaking glass, and a disturbing blue flickering fire showed through its portholes. Getting stronger and stronger . . .

Prepoc swung back towards the spoilheaps as the Wawaka's nerve finally broke.

They ran up towards the cairn, hampered by their weapons, slipping and stumbling blindly on the tussocks of grass.

Prepoc waited calmly till he could get three with one shot. They vanished from the earth, picked as neatly from the tussocks as a swallow catches a butterfly on the wing.

The last Wawaka saw Prepoc. But it was stumbling and out of breath; its blast missed him by yards, cutting a swath among the dead crows on the far side of the cairn.

Prepoc did not miss. Then, with a long shot, he put the self-maimed Wawaka that still lay writhing on the spoilheaps out of its misery.

Prepoc nearly died then; for as he watched, with satisfaction, the upturned mirror-ship vaporize in a white flash that seared the heather for a hundred yards around, two more mirror-ships materialized, directly overhead.

Who, wondered Prepoc, had been foolish enough to give the silly Wawaka the gift of time-travel?

After that, Ralph really ceased to exist, except as a body that leapt and rolled and spun, and whose finger worked the blaster.

Prepoc, hero, leader, warrior, was fighting his last battle.

The countryside stirred in its sleep. Below the ridge, in sight of home, the two collies, not even singed, cowered in the deepest part of the burn. Their ears were flattened, their tails down. They whined and huddled together, seeking the warmth and comfort of each other in a world they no longer recognized. Their lips were permanently back, exposing their yellow fangs in a silent snarl that had long since ceased to have any meaning for them. Occasionally, when the world grew quiet for a moment, they would relax enough to lap water furtively. But they never stopped shivering; never dared to poke their heads out and see what was happening. Then the ear-hurting noises and blinding flashes would start again.

But they would not desert their master.

Down in the valley, Mam stirred in her sleep, and looked up to see, through the curtained window, the flashes up on the fell. She listened to the thunder rolling continuously.

'Glad Ralph's not out in that,' she thought, and went back to sleep.

At Fylingdales Moor, the radar-operators reported strange blips on their smaller sets; the ones that were not trained on Russia. Even the bigger sets showed a worrying tendency to fuzz. The operators pressed the minor alarm-buzzers at their elbow, summoning maintenance-technicians, who in turn summoned duty-officers, who in turn rang higher duty-officers. But after a while, when nothing more threatening developed, they just logged 'Severe electrical storm over northern Pennines' and went back to watching for Ivan.

Only Ruby knew what it was. All night she watched the flashings from her window, hugging the family cat for comfort. The cat was tense; its claws penetrated the thin stuff of her old sprigged nightdress painfully, but even that seemed to ease her agony.

When the noise faded, she allowed herself to hope a little. Then came a last boom, without any flash in the sky, and she said:

'Oh, Ralph, you silly bugger,' and went on staring desperately up the hillside.

Prepoc had found these new Wawaka annoyingly hard to kill; they had learnt new tricks from somewhere. He had disabled both mirrorships. One had blown up, and the other wasn't long for this universe. But its crew had escaped. He had fought them all night, using every trick he knew, and there were still four of them left. They knew all *his* tricks now; and there were only two blasts left in his once inexhaustible blaster . . .

It looked like the end. He was not at all worried for himself; he had always wished to die in battle. But he hated leaving a job unfinished . . . untidy.

Slowly he wormed his way through the heather. His body was weak and tired. It had felt weak and tired from the beginning; weak and clumsy and slow. That had been half the trouble. He could not leap and climb like he used to. The claws of this body were short, blunt and useless . . . almost non-existent.

It was time to hide in the earth. Something drew him into the bowels of the earth, something told him there was vast new strength down there, if he could reach it. Strange . . .

He came to the opening he had sensed, the opening he was looking for. A narrow fissure in the sandstone, a dark deep place. He crept in painfully, backwards, keeping his eyes always to the front.

At first the going was difficult; narrow sharp turns up and down, left and right, that he could hardly worm round, in his newfound stiffness of limb. A nightmare, when he had to hold the blaster always ready. But the deeper he got, the better the going got . . . almost straight, almost as if made by some intelligent species . . .

If the Wawaka followed him in . . . perhaps he could get all four with one shot. That would be a satisfactory thing to do, before he died. But . . . they wouldn't be that stupid. They would wait outside, bottling him up, till they could bring up one of their big machines which could blast deep through the rock, and lift him out a helpless prisoner . . .

No. They were coming. They weren't waiting for their big

machine. Foolish, foolish! What could be drawing them on to their deaths? He had only to wait quietly . . .

He settled himself; took a little of the remaining green paste and waited, patient as a cat at a mouse-hole; but still worried about what could be drawing the Wawaka so needlessly to their deaths. Even Wawaka were not usually *that* foolish.

He waited till the first was nearly on him.

He got all four with one shot.

Satisfied, he pushed up his helmet-visor.

The little tendrils retracted. Ralph returned to a brief flicker of consciousness. Then he fainted. Or slept the sleep of utter exhaustion.

CHAPTER 17

He wakened in a blackness so black he couldn't believe it. He kept
blinking and wiping his eyes, as if to clear away a layer of black soot
that clung there.

Had he gone blind? Had the Wawaka caught him? Was the grey
mould growing over his eyeballs?

But his eyes felt just the same as usual, only sore. Then his hand
came into contact with the helmet he was still wearing. He pulled
down the visor, hoping it would pierce the darkness, as it had pierced
the darkness of the fell at night.

Nothing. Still darkness. Except . . . a tiny red mark in the darkness.
Like the branch of a red tree. Was it just the shape of some nerve in
his eyeball? The last dying flicker of sight?

He tried to move towards it. He could barely crawl; every muscle
of his body, and some he didn't even know he had, screamed in
separate agony. What had beaten him up? His body felt pulled to
pieces. But he crawled.

The mark got bigger, and wobbled about as he moved. He wasn't
blind; just crawling in total darkness. He became aware of his knees
and the palms of his hands. They were moving across a surface
smooth as glass. A curved surface that extended up on each side
and met about a foot over his head.

He was crawling inside some smooth pipe, about four feet in
diameter. Horror at being trapped inside a pipe swept over him. But
every pipe must have an end. There *must* be a way out . . . he
continued towards the red tree.

Then the visor banged against rock.

The red tree was a glowing crack in the black rock.

He tore at the rock with his hands; it came away easily. But
beyond was a smooth, glassy, glowing red surface that he couldn't
even make a scratch on. He couldn't *see* anything through the red,
glassy surface, either. Dead end.

He lay, holding lumps of the crumbling rock in either hand. In his

122

numbing terror, he crumbled the rocks to dust that ran out between his fingers and left nothing.

He must turn and go the other way. But there was only darkness that way, not even the red glow. Suppose he found the other end blocked, too? Or suppose he was down one of the lead-mines? They were *mazes*. You could take a wrong turning and get lost in the dark for ever, crawling further and further from the light until you could crawl no further and died. Some of the old miners had taken the wrong turn down some natural crack and never been found . . .

He lay whimpering to himself. What was the point of moving at all?

And then, in the silence between two whimpers, he heard . . .

Snuffing. Like a dog snuffing. He listened and lost it; listened and heard it again.

Wawaka?

He kept utterly still; tried to not even breathe. Even if he still had Prepoc's blaster, it must be thirty yards down the tunnel, down towards where the snuffing was coming from. All he could do was lie and try not to breathe.

Then came a whine; a little, short, querulous, timid whine. And he knew who'd made it . . .

'C'mere, Nance!' he shouted.

Nance set up a tremendous volley of barking, that rang and echoed in the pipe. Then Jet was barking with her. Their barks were full of loneliness and half-forgotten terror, but they sounded like the music of heaven . . . He felt Nance come up to him slowly, crawling on her belly, feeling her way in the dark with her forepaws thrust out trembling before her. Then she was in Ralph's arms, and her glad barking was lost in licking and snuffling and wriggling.

They had come and found him. I know my sheepdogs and am known of them! And where they had got in, perhaps he could get out. Or at least they could go for help, and he could be dug out, as fox-hunters dig out a terrier trapped underground.

Finally, he nerved himself to try it. 'Ga wey, Nance! Ga wey, Jet!' And he heard them in front, scrabbling nervously onwards.

The rock grew rough under his hands. Sloped steeply upwards. Then, just as suddenly fell into a hole, so that his hands landed on nothing, and his chest hit the floor with a lung-whooshing thump, and he nearly fell headfirst.

But a little draught of cool fresh air came up that hole, and, from the depths, an encouraging bark from Jet.

He lowered himself from darkness into darkness.

It seemed to go on for ever. But all the time the little draught of air grew stronger. And at last, a grey light crept down the tunnel towards him, glinting off the damp rocks as off a diamond . . .

He shoved his head out, like a rabbit from a burrow, and saw the dim curve of the fellside. It was still night, but after the black darkness, it seemed as bright as day. He sucked in great lungfuls of fell-smell.

He had been down a lead-mine; in the middle of the night. How the hell had he *got* there? Then it all came flooding back; a confused blur of mirror-ships falling and the blaze of Wawaka's blasters . . .

Were they all gone?

Jet and Nance would not have come where there were Wawaka. And there they were, out on the open heather, sitting and scratching themselves, as if nothing had ever happened . . . he was safe.

And in that moment he remembered the red glass wall underground; and his old stubborn curiosity overcame him.

He tried to tell himself to be sensible. It would be best to get home and get cleaned up and into bed before Mam wakened up.

But he must know about the red glow. Besides, he'd left the blaster and the red egg and the radiation-bag somewhere down there. He must fetch them . . .

The collies watched, baffled, as he vanished back down the hole from which they'd just rescued him. They cocked their heads and then, with reluctant whines, followed him back in.

It didn't seem so far, going back. Soon he lay shaking and panting in the smooth pipe again, the blaster in his hand, and the red, glowing, glassy wall in front. Jet and Nance came snuffling up behind. He pushed them well back, before he aimed the blaster at the red wall. He didn't know what effect it would have in this confined space.

In the flare of the blaster, the red wall showed up as yellow metal: Fefethil-metal. And he understood that the smooth pipe he had been crawling in was a hole bored by his own blaster; that last blast that had killed the four Wawaka with one shot . . .

He saw the new blast carve a smooth round hole in the yellow metal wall. Then the blast was finished, and sooty darkness returned.

He crawled up to the hole he had made. The sides were cool and

124

smooth. He felt beyond, and his fingers touched a smooth, glassy floor. He cautiously crawled through.

More sooty dark, in which he could at least stand upright. Cool dry air, moving against his skin.

And that same safe, antiseptic smell that had come from Prepoc's coffin . . . His skin *crawled*. A Fefethil room, underground; far underground. And the smell of undecaying death . . .

Had he found the tomb of Sephotic?

Then a blue light flicked on overhead, making him jump out of his skin. And another, further off. And another.

He'd once seen a mouse emerge from a hole in the skirting-board at home. A mouse that had gazed paralysed at the immensity of chairs and tables and Mam doing the ironing and the blue sky and moving clouds outside the window . . .

He felt like that mouse now. He was in a domed hall . . . the only thing he could compare it to was St Paul's Cathedral, visited on that school trip to London. Only this place was twice the size . . . The roof glowed blue like the night sky, and twinkled with living constellations. But they were not stars Ralph knew. He looked for the Plough and the Pole Star, and they were not there.

And the floor was polished like a mirror, mirroring the domed roof of stars into a bottomless pit of stars into which he could fall for ever.

And then the music started. It didn't come from any one place; it came from everywhere. And it was so sad that Ralph could have wept. One tear did roll down his cheek, but he wiped it away with a savage movement of his ripped anorak sleeve. He knew it was Fefethil-music; it sounded like Theloc talking, when he was at his saddest. But its sadness *fed* him, more than laughter.

He waited for someone to come. He waited a long time and no one came. Then he realized no one would ever come, and walked forwards towards the two giant statues he would ever afterwards think of as the Weepers. A huge pair of cats facing each other, carved in a black stone with a soft blue sheen; cats sitting on pedestals, with their great heads bowed over stiffened forelegs, so that each looked at its own reflection in the mirror-floor.

He passed between them; beyond, there was a whole avenue of them. He kept walking across the mirror-floor, half-frightened of slipping and falling down into that mirror-universe for ever. He stopped and looked down into it, and saw his own face looking up at him, wrinkled and foreshortened. I look like a ragged old ape, he thought ruefully. An old and wrinkled ape. That is how I'll look when I'm old . . .

Then he saw, with horror, a piece of mud crack away from his caked boots, and fall on the shining mirror-floor. And when he looked behind he saw a whole trail of mud, leading back to the round blaster-hole and the friendly faces of the two bewildered collies peering through.

'Sorry,' he shouted, to no one in particular. 'Sorry, sorry, sorry' his voice came echoing back. He felt more guilty about the mud than anything he'd ever done in his life. He stooped and tried to pick it up. But the stooping made more mud crack off his boots. And then he trampled on a bit and it smeared to a brown stain, an ugly brown stain on the mirror-stars. And the more he tried to clear it up, the more mess he made . . .

Then there was a little sigh in the air; a little mechanical sigh, and the mud began to vanish, starting at the round dark hole. and working slowly towards his feet. When it was all miraculously gone, he shouted 'Sorry' again.

There was no answer; but no anger either. He walked on, looking back every so often to see the trail of mud he was still making vanishing behind him.

Each pair of Weepers was exactly the same; each Weeper had a collar with a great golden sunburst hanging round its neck. And on their bases was writing, gold symbols he couldn't understand. It reminded him of something. He couldn't think what, until he remembered the village war-memorial.

The avenue of Weepers ended; he had come to a crossroads. Great halls ran off into darkness, left and right.

Another hall ran on ahead. It was black, without stars; but in the blackness a great box of glass glowed dim gold.

Three dead bodies lay inside the box, with their feet towards him. Huge dead bodies, twice the size of his own. Their massive dark-grey limbs shone like gun-metal, contorted into grotesque positions as if they had just died, and died horribly. They too had once walked upright, like Wawaka and Fefethil and apes. But their feet ended in a horny double-claw. And they had tails, thick and round as gun-barrels, with a pointed barb like a poisoned arrowhead at the end of them.

Their chests were massive, humped like small mountains; the chest-muscles brutally strong and covered with gun-metal scales.

Ralph was afraid to look at their faces, but he had to look in the end.

They had the faces of men; infinitely brutal men, with flattened noses, thick massive cheekbones, and oddly high foreheads from which stubby horns grew, like a young calf's horns just budding. And their long, gun-metal eyes were open in death, glinting darkly in the shadows of their massive eyebrow-arches, so that you couldn't tell if they were looking at you or not. But wherever they seemed to look, they looked with hate and malice that foretold the end of all living things.

The Lords of the Attock.

They were also . . . the Devil . . . the horns, the cloven hoofs, the forked tails. All they lacked was pitchforks . . .

But they still held blasters; and the blasters splayed out into three points at the end . . .

Ralph's mind reeled. Mam's favourite bit of the Bible! Revelation, chapter XII.

'And there was war in heaven. Michael and his angels fought against the dragon. And the dragon fought, and his angels, and prevailed not. Neither was their place found any more in heaven. And the great dragon was cast out, that old serpent called the Devil . . . he was cast out into the earth, and his angels were cast out with him . . .'

When had the Book of Revelation been written? When the Romans, the red helmets, had ruled Britain; and that's when Theloc said the Attock were overthrown.

Had the author of Revelation watched the final hunting-down of the Attock? Was the Bible *all* true, just twisted a bit in the telling? Was this the Foul Fiend of the Pit?

This mountain was called Fiend's Fell . . .

And, in spite of the technical skill of the Fefethil, was some poison still leaking out of this case, from the Attock bodies? A poison that drove poor apes mad, so that they slaughtered each other in millions . . . Lebanon and El Salvador, Vietnam and Iran?

Bewildered, Ralph blundered on. But not till he had made sure, from another inspection of their blaster-shattered rib-cages, that the Lords of the Attock were really and truly dead, beyond any danger of resurrection.

Far ahead, another glass box lit up suddenly in the blackness. Ralph walked towards it, nervously. It was oddly like walking down to the lit-up telephone kiosk at Unthank on a dark night. But this was a hundred times bigger than any telephone kiosk.

It contained a complete lump of heather-covered hillside. The heather actually looked alive and growing. On it was built a cairn, like the cairn on the fell; but the cairn's stones looked new, freshly quarried. Beside the cairn was a glass coffin, like the one Prepoc had been buried in. It was open, and inside lay a striped furry body.

It had to be Sephotic. He lay peacefully on his side, as Prepoc had done. But he was smaller than Prepoc, and looked older; white hairs round his muzzle. And somehow, in spite of the blaster his hand rested on, he looked as if he'd never been much of a warrior. There was a feeling of weakness and vanity; Ralph knew the Fefethil face pretty well by then.

Sephotic, whose jealousy of Prepoc had caused all the trouble.

He looked peaceful enough now.

Glancing beyond him, Ralph saw he had reached a dead-end. He walked back to the crossroads, just stopping to make sure again that the Lords of the Attock hadn't stirred.

He stepped into the darkness of one of the cross-halls.

Immediately, it lit up. But this light was a fiery red. And the music changed. Martial music now, that tautened his weary body and made him walk tall, as if he'd taken a fingertip of green paste . . .

This red hall was even bigger than the others. Here, the great ships hung, on their sparkling force-fields, looking bigger than the QE2 in dry dock. Hatches hung open, beneath their golden bellies, and from them hung smaller ships; the golden fighting-ships of the Fefethil that he'd last seen hovering in the sky on tails of flame, the day he put on Prepoc's fun-helmet, so long ago.

Half the fleet that destroyed the Attock must be here. But there were also small, beautiful things, laid out on tables of what looked like solid glass. This simple shining ball, looking so harmless and peaceful, with beautifully engraved decoration that swirled like clouds all over its surface. A thing so lovely he could not resist picking it up . . .

Next instant, its surface had turned into a hundred crawling golden spiders; tiny metal spiders that ran up over his hands and arms and into his hair.

But as he stood, too paralysed even to scream, they all ran out of his hair again, down his arms and over his hands, and vanished back into the swirling patterns of the golden ball, which became exactly as before.

He put it down, sweating. It had looked a gift fit for a prince. Some princeling of the Attock? Designed, perhaps, to be picked up as booty in the Attock plundering of some world, and taken back to the Attock royal court. No doubt the spiders were deadly poison. How many Attock princelings had they killed? The infinitely cunning mind of Sephotic . . .

It had not killed him, because he was not Attock. But it reminded him this was a living fleet, not a dead memorial . . . and it cured him of further meddling. He walked across the crossroads to the last hall. It too lit up red; more fighting-ships.

The first ship wasn't gold. It hung battered and black, scored and pitted from a hundred battles . . .

This must be Prepoc's ship. As he approached, the cockpit-cover swung slowly open, as if in greeting, and a short golden ladder descended. It seemed like some weary old collie wagging its tail to greet a beloved master. Tears pricked at Ralph's eyes, before he realized it must be responding to Prepoc's helmet, which he was still wearing.

He felt impelled to climb aboard; to get near Prepoc for the last time. He sank into what seemed a very comfortable seat . . .

The seat wriggled beneath him, until it fitted his bottom and back to perfection. A safety-belt clamped snugly round his waist. The instrument panel lit up, throwing strange indecipherable glowing patterns on the windscreen in front of his face.

Then his helmet's visor snapped down of its own accord. Tentacles came from the sides of the cockpit, as well as the sides of the helmet. For a moment, he felt he was being strangled, then all was peace. He and the ship were one.

But he was still Ralph. Prepoc did not invade him and push him out of the driving-seat. Perhaps the helmet was running down, losing power. Certainly it could not overcome his will, though Prepoc was still there in his mind.

What had this ship done, he wondered? Where had it been, in the great universe? If only it could tell what it had seen . . . that last great battle when Brunitaj, the world of the Attock, was destroyed . . .

Instantly, he was in black space. The whole fleet, great ships and small, was around him. The cloud of Attock destructor-scouts was flying at him, like a cloud of silver midges. They were coming very fast, but they dodged erratically from side to side, with the same maddening, meaningless, maze-like dance that midges had. They vanished and reappeared, blinking in and out of time. It was impossible to aim at any one of them; let alone hit one. His mind despaired. And then, from the mother-ship on his right, beams of red light shot out, and began to circle like the beams of a great lighthouse in the sky, like a great cartwheel, taking in all space. And not only all space, but all time in that space.

Caught in the wheeling, circling beams, the Attock destructor-scouts glowed like sparks and died. Sephotic's last great weapon had worked; there were jubilant murmurs into Ralph's headphones from all the fleet. Then the whole fleet changed course to the right. And Brunitaj swam into view. A brown world; brown oceans with skeins of brown islands and a few small, fat continents.

It grew in size with enormous swiftness, like a brown flower opening. He watched the islands multiply and magnify in that brown, brown sea. Like lines of bubbles in gravy; like skeins of brown lace.

A dry voice came over the headphones now; a creaking dry voice that tried to seem calm, yet trembled with excitement. Ralph knew it must be Sephotic's voice, trembling with the prospect of final victory. Yet all it did was count down from ten to one, in the strange Fefethil language.

And then silvery torpedo-shapes detached themselves from all the fleet. And the fleet stopped dead, with a crushing deceleration that made him feel his brains were coming out of his ears, his nose, his mouth. As if his eyeballs were about to leap out of their sockets, and the comfortable safety-belt cut him in half like a sword. As if he was about to be sprayed in a bloody mess all over the inside of his own cockpit windows.

Then perfect stillness and silence, as the fleet held its breath, and the silvery torpedoes seemed to vanish into the bulk of Brunitaj.

A long wait, and nothing happening, except the harshness of Sephotic's breathing. After a long time, Sephotic began counting again. If he had been trembling before, he was much worse now.

Two. One. Zero.

And then circular ripples expanding in the seas of Brunitaj; spreading as ripples do in a pond when a boy throws a stone in, only much more slowly. But these ripples, as they met and crossed, wiped out whole skeins of islands as if they were no more than floating duckweed.

130

And then Brunitaj turned white and grew a little. And Ralph knew those seas had mixed with the inner fires, and turned to steam. Great fiery flashes in the steam, that curdled and whirled round the white mass. Then Brunitaj quietened down and simply turned in space, a pink, milky ball; and Ralph knew it was all over.

'Good,' said Sephotic. 'I feared there might be a chain-reaction, and it would turn into a nova . . .'

'One ship escaped,' came a computer-voice. 'Small, lightly-armed, very fast.'

The red joy of the hunt flared in Prepoc's mind . . .

Then the vision faded, and Ralph found himself sitting in the red hall again.

But a change was coming over the whole fleet. The fighting-ships were retracting into the mother-ships; all but Prepoc's own. And on the mother-ships, rows of lights were coming on; hatchways were closing. The whole fleet was alive, getting ready for something . . .

For what? Voices came into his headphones; voices of long-dead Fefethil captains, from the memory banks of their long-dark battle-computers. Apathoc and Memeroc and Lefeloc, who survived alone in the last battle of Philot . . . Again they lived, hungry for battle. A ghost-fleet, ready to sail. A ghost-fleet with all its dreadful power intact. A ghost-fleet whose power could never be equalled now, even by the Fefethil.

But sail where to?

They could only be waiting for *his* orders. There was no other living being here. Ralph slowly realized, with sweating palms, that, like all the arch-villains in all the rubbish sci-fi films he'd ever watched, he had the power to conquer the universe. And the long-silent battle-computers pressed harder and harder on his mind, demanding orders . . .

The Wawaka? Settle the Wawaka once and for all? It seemed the only sensible thing to do . . . then maybe we could come back to earth, and frighten some sense into all the horrible presidents and politicians and prime ministers and terrorists who were killing so many people . . . apartheid . . .

He heard himself sniggering nervously. It wasn't a very pretty sound, to be made by a potential conqueror of the universe . . .

The voice of the Sephotic-computer came again. 'We have located the dispositions of the Wawaka battle-fleets. They are very crude and primitive . . . I suggest that . . .'

131

The Wawaka didn't have a prayer. The final solution to the Wawaka problem was at hand. Ralph couldn't stop the sniggering; it sounded to his own ears like the sniggering of a madman.

'But first you must eliminate the current Fefethil fleet. They will attempt to intercept you. Their advance scout is within five thousand miles of this world. Commander is Theloc . . . We must eliminate the ship of Theloc now before we take off . . .'

Ralph thought of Theloc and Thmeses, Huthme and Huthmir . . . He couldn't do it.

'Oh, *shit!*' said Ralph, and pushed up the visor of the helmet in a rage. Slowly, another change came over the great fleet. The voices went silent; the rows of lights dimmed; the hatches reopened and the fighting-ships returned to their original positions. Even the hall's red light seemed to dim; the martial music faded, and Ralph found himself just feeling very weary and shivering with cold. With a nasty echo of 'Final solution of the Wawaka problem' fading in his mind.

Hitler had wanted a final solution for the Jews.

He walked back down the blue hall, his teeth chattering, feeling he had just escaped going clean out of his mind, in the nastiest kind of way.

The sight of Nance and Jet, still peering through the round blaster-hole, seemed the best sight in the world then. He sent them crawling ahead down the tunnel, and tried to close the round hole he'd made, with a reverse blast of his blaster.

But the blaster only made a funny, fizzing sound, and he found he couldn't make it work any more. He felt naked without it. But he bunged it into the radiation-bag with the helmet and the egg, and slung the bag over his shoulder by the piece of old washing-line. Then he crawled after the dogs, feeling as low as he'd ever done in his life.

CHAPTER 18

Dawn was breaking, as he emerged a second time.

He looked up towards the cairn, and gasped. The fellside was gutted; as if a dozen giant bulldozers had had a drunken orgy. Sharp-edged gullies crossed and recrossed each other. The water from the burns had filled them; new waterfalls ran down sheer peat-faces, already wearing them away into runnels.

There was no repairing it; no hiding it. From the sky it must be as visible as Manchester Airport. Let alone the radiation it must be giving off ...

Worse, the devastation reached right down from the cairn to the mouth of the lead-mine he'd just left. And there it stopped. The land beyond was normal. From the sky, the scars must look like a giant hand, pointing its finger at the lead-mine. Prepoc, in his last frenzy, had led the Wawaka to the very door of Sephotic's tomb. Now it was theirs for the taking.

He turned back to the mouth of the lead-mine. There were a few loose boulders lying around the foot of the little crag. Heaving and straining, gasping and moaning, he stuffed them into the hole. It wasn't a big hole, no more than any lead-mine entrance was. But even when he'd used up all the boulders, the top two inches of darkness still gaped at him, like a dreadful sin, like a deadly wound. He tried pulling the tufts of heather down over it; but the heather just sprang back into place.

And what about the evidence up top, round the cairn? He climbed up the devastation very slowly, dreading what he might see. Especially what the crows had done to Prepoc ...

But there was blessedly little. The places where the mirror-ships had exploded were just huge burned circles, full of charred heather-stems that drew black marks on his boots and trousers. The cairn itself was gone, blasted right out of existence by a criss-cross of gullies; only a few odd stones remained.

The coffin was gone too, and the body of Prepoc. Even of the dead crows there was little sign but vast drifts of black feathers, that stirred with a soft rustling sound in the first of the morning wind as if, cheated of life, they strove to return.

He was glad; at least Prepoc would not be stuffed now, and put in some museum. He wondered if Theloc had come already, and tidied up as best he could. But Prepoc's body could just have disappeared in the fury of the fighting . . . His weary mind boggled at the endless possibilities, and gave up. He would never know what had happened for sure.

The morning was grey and dull; a heavy rain began to fall, drenching him to the skin. At least it would wash some of the radiation off him. But he felt hopeless, hopeless. And very scared in a dreary way. He, alone in the universe, knew all about the tomb of Sephotic. The Wawaka would never leave him alone now.

He felt so *alone*. Except for Jet and Nance. And they were soaked and cowering. He must get them home quick or they might get ill, after what they'd been through. But they looked at him with their faithful brown eyes, and wagged their tails feebly and licked his hand. Tears scalded from his eyes. Alone . . .

'Ra-alph!'

The dogs were not the only faithful ones. Way down the fellside, struggling like a drowning fly amidst the newly formed gullies, was a thin, muddy figure in an old green anorak. Ralph just knew from the way she walked that she was still wearing unsuitable shoes. But there was a bulging rucksack on her shoulder . . .

He struggled down to meet her, as fast as he could move. He grabbed her in an enormous bear-hug full of rucksack and mud, rain and pain. But it shut out the cold and the dark and the loneliness. They stood a long time, teetering dangerously on the edge of a new waterfall, with the peat crumbling away underneath their feet.

Then he looked at her face; it was shiny with rain, and her nose was red, and her long hair hung in rats'-tails from under a sodden bobble-cap. But her eyes looked at nothing in the world but him. There seemed to be nothing in the world but him. It filled him with embarrassment. He wasn't *that* important. Yet it made him feel good as well.

'I've brought you some coffee,' she said. 'I thought you were dead.' Then, looking around she said, 'Haven't you made a mess?' as if he'd left his bedroom untidy, or dropped a jar of jam. Then she burst into tears.

He couldn't bear the importance of it all; he was too tired. So he said, as cheerfully as he could, 'Let's have some coffee, then. I'm *starved.*'

She opened the rucksack. There wasn't just coffee; there were sandwiches wrapped in foil, a first-aid kit and a big, black plastic bag.

'What's the plastic bag for?'

'In case you were . . . dead. To pick up the . . . bits. They use plastic bags for dead people . . .' She was crying helplessly again. He thought what it must have cost her, to come up here. Afraid of the Wawaka, afraid of him being dead. But she'd come. She hadn't even had a helmet or a blaster. He thought she was much braver than him. He told her so, haltingly and shiveringly.

'Oh yeah,' she said, wiping her face with a muddy sleeve. 'And now I *am* here, I go on like a wet lettuce.' He put his arms round her again, and she snuggled into his armpit like she was a rabbit digging a burrow. 'Oh, you do *smell* nice,' she said in a muffled voice.

They were still standing there when a blatting sound broke in on them. A little scout helicopter, all spidery metalwork and a glass bubble on the front; painted dark green, with ARMY and a whole string of numerals along the side. Nobody waved from it; it flew back and forth inspecting them as if they were no more than flies, then landed out of sight beyond where the cairn had been.

'Don't say much,' said Ralph. 'Just tell them what you saw walking up here this morning. We came up together, right? As soon as it was light, to see if the sheep were OK. Let me do the talking.'

They walked up the fell again. Ralph didn't know how his legs managed it. His soaked trousers were starting to chafe the inside of his thighs raw.

'Who are you, kid?' asked the sergeant who came to meet them. He was a para with a red beret and camouflage jacket, but he looked a bit dazed. Dazed and angry at the same time. 'What the hell's been going on round here? You got the early-warning radar shot to hell!'

'Dunno.' Ralph played it stupid, which wasn't hard with his teeth chattering so much. 'Big thunderstorm last night. Came to see if any of my sheep had been killed. I'm the shepherd.'

'And how many sheep have been killed?' The sergeant seemed desperate for facts; *any* facts.

Ralph was struck dumb. But Ruby said quickly, 'We ain't seen none dead. They're all down by the fence, just dead-scared.'

'Who's she?' asked the sergeant.

'Girlfriend. Came up wi' me.'

'What's your names?' asked the sergeant even more desperately, pulling a notebook out of a camouflaged pocket down by his knee. He wrote down their names, ages, occupations, employers . . . then tore off the sheet and handed it to the other man inside the helicopter. They listened silently as the pilot relayed all their private details to an authoritative squawking voice that said things like 'I copy you'. They spoke queerly, all X-rays and Bravos, fifers and niners. The sergeant's eyes roamed wildly round the fellside. He kept saying, 'God what a mess' and 'Jesus H. Christ' in a totally pointless way. The radio squawked again, and he said to Ralph:

'Stand by – CO's on his way.' That seemed to make him feel a lot better. 'What's in your bag, kid?'

Ralph grabbed at the radiation-bag wildly. 'Me gear – me shepherding things.'

'What – a shepherd's crook, like?'

Ralph nearly burst out laughing; they hadn't used shepherd's crooks since Granda's day. But the long shape of the blaster took some accounting for, so he just said 'Yeah. And me butties, and a jar o' Stockholm tar.'

The sergeant turned his attention to the two collies, who were sniffing the helicopter's landing-skids and peeing on them. 'Must be a quiet life, being a shepherd. Not a lot of action, eh?'

'Would you like some coffee?' asked Ruby helpfully. The two soldiers drank all the coffee, ate most of the sandwiches, made friends with the dogs and asked Ralph how much money he made a week.

Then there was more blatting in the sky, and there appeared six huge Chinook helicopters coming in, line-ahead. Instantly the sergeant was gabbling questions to Ralph about safe landing-sites and sink-holes and bogs, and there was more fifering and ninering on the radio. Then the sergeant waved his arms like a cricket-umpire, standing where the cairn had been, and the Chinooks landed one by one well clear of trouble. And streams of little brown figures came bubbling out of them, carrying guns and bent double, and covered the whole fellside in a fast-running wave; ending in a great circle round the devastated area, lying on the ground with their weapons pointing outwards. Pretty smooth and impressive, if you forgot the way Prepoc moved. Prepoc could have had this lot for breakfast . . .

'What did you say, kid?' asked the sergeant.

'Nothing,' mumbled Ralph.

Another helicopter landed, marked UKAEA Sellafield. Civilians with yellow safety-helmets and yellow oilskin coats, with boxes slung over their backs, started apparently vacuuming the burnt heather. The boxes on their backs began rattling vigorously.

'Geiger counters,' said the sergeant importantly. 'Sounds pretty radioactive to me. Baffling, innit?'

'Mebbe it was flying saucers,' suggested Ralph helpfully.

The sergeant gave him a professionally pitying look.

Then a group of officers came across. The biggest had a strip saying Major Martineau on the left breast of his camouflage jacket.

'Get these civilian personnel cleared off-site, sergeant. Pronto!'

'This is the lad who found it, sir. He reckons it might be flying saucers.'

All the officers raised their eyebrows pityingly. Ralph thought it was great; as soon as you mentioned flying saucers people discounted you as the village idiot.

'Have these people checked for radioactivity and fly them home. Don't want people saying they caught pneumonia while in the army's care.'

The Geiger counter flicked over the radiation-bag, while Ralph stood tensely holding his breath. But scratched and battered though it was, the radiation-bag still worked; not a rattle. His soaking clothes rattled a bit, but little more than Ruby's. Thank God for this endless drenching rain ... His left wrist made the Geiger rattle like hell, making him jump. But the man in yellow simply pulled up his sleeve, exposing his luminous wrist-watch.

'They'll live,' said the man in the yellow coat, dismissively. 'Have a good bath and wash your clothes when you get home.'

The helicopter trip was over almost before it began. Ralph cuddled Ruby with one hand, and stroked the dogs with the other, and persuaded the pilot that the top end of Jack Norton's bottom field was the best landing-site. So he just had time to store the radiation-bag in the lead-mine before the first villagers came running up ... Then it was all hot baths and whisky and talk, talk, talk, until the first reporters came.

Mam sold Ralph's story exclusive for three hundred pounds. She sold it four times over, to four separate papers, during the course of the day. 'Make hay while the sun shines,' she said darkly. 'Cos it's a long time rainin'.' Ralph and Ruby, Jet and Nance were photographed from every possible angle. They even made Ralph get Granda's old shepherd's crook down off the chimney-breast and pose with that. Then they discovered Ruby had nice legs . . .

Then the television-vans arrived . . .

The army sealed off the fell for a distance of half a mile, on every side of the smashed-up area. The TV men got out their telephoto lenses, or hired helicopters, and got excellent footage of the gouges in the fellside, and the soldiers guarding them . . .

But next day, bafflingly, nothing appeared in the papers, or on telly. In the afternoon the police came round, saying what was going on up the fell was just army manoeuvres . . . the Royal Engineers were trying out a new way of carving landing-strips for Harrier jump-jets out of mountainous terrain. Any farmer who suffered damage to his land would be fully compensated, right away . . .

Two officers with red on their caps came to see Jack Norton. Jack, who had been holding forth on the iniquity of the government gagging the press with D-notices, suddenly went very quiet. But he actually stood a round of drinks in the pub at Melmerby that same night, an unheard-of event. And next day everybody knew he had ordered a Vauxhall Carlton from the agency at Penrith, to replace his awful old banger. Some people reckoned the army had *bought* the fell off him . . .

The next day he sent Ralph to bring the sheep down.

Ralph had hoped to get a good look at what was going on; but the sheep were still huddled by the bottom fence, being guarded by paras with rifles. The rest of the fell seethed with men putting up coils of barbed wire. Bulldozers had carved out a car-park, that was already turning to a sea of black mud, in which sat many tracked vehicles with twenty-foot aerials. There were Portakabins and Portaloos, and a huge sign saying 'Western Command. Experimental site. Danger. Do not enter when the red flag is flying.' There were red flags all over the place . . . It should have been very impressive, but it just reminded Ralph of the brainless way ants rushed about when your foot broke into their nest . . .

He kept looking up towards the little crag of rock. He could see it quite clearly; he even fancied he could see the two-inch hole he'd left, gaping like a wound, gaping like a sin . . . Once the army stopped panicking, they'd certainly see it.

'Wotcher want, kid?' asked the sentry, from behind a red-and-white striped barrier. Ralph was handed on to the sergeant of the guard, then the duty officer, then to Major Martineau who whirled him into a Portakabin where a very high officer indeed sat.

'Get those damned animals out of here,' said the officer, glaring at Nance and Jet. He had the coldest, palest, blue eyes Ralph had ever seen. He rapped out questions at Ralph, and didn't even wait to hear the answers. Ralph was frightened of being caught out at first; then he realized the officer didn't want to *know* anything; he just wanted to make Ralph feel small . . . like those huntsmen on horses who came in all their grandeur to hunt foxes that were no bigger than a cat. Foxes that did a useful job clearing the fell of carrion, and never took a lamb that wasn't sick or dying. Ralph always refused to open gates for the hunt; and he often felt the huntsmen would have liked to punish his insolence by giving him a cut across the face with their riding-crops . . . Ralph hated huntsmen nearly as much as he hated crows.

As the officer went on, making him feel small by asking pointless questions about the sheep and the fell, a change came over Ralph. He began to see the officer as Theloc would have seen him; as a murderous ape. All his life, since he first learnt to switch on the black-and-white telly at the age of three, there'd been these murderous apes in camouflage jackets, killing, killing, killing. Vietnam and Biafra, Lebanon and Nicaragua.

And if they spotted that gap in the rocks they'd be spilling out into the universe, riding in Prepoc's fleet. Already they'd turned space into a rubbish-tip with their satellite junk. But what they could do with Prepoc's fleet didn't bear thinking about. He'd rather the Wawaka got it . . .

But at least while the army was there, the Wawaka might stay away . . . or would they come anyway, and there'd be a final battle royal between murderous Wawaka and murderous apes?

He must contact Theloc, quick. Before something terrible happened. But how?

He came back to the present, to find he hadn't answered the officer's last two questions . . .

'Boy's a total fool,' said the officer. 'Get him and his bloody sheep out from under my feet pronto, Martineau . . .'

He finally got the sheep down the green-road to Pasture House, with the help of Jet and Nance and a lot of over-eager, clumsy paras.

139

When they got there, Jack Norton was waiting by the open gate; and the field was full of new drinking-troughs and dozens of bales of new hay.

The army *must* have given Jack a lot of money . . .

CHAPTER 19

Pasture House lay just below the Alston road, as it climbed Hartside Height. In the old days, before people expected tap-water and flush toilets, it had been a hill-farm. It was still intact, with its thick sandstone walls and sagging roof. The middle section was a great barn. At one end was a byre for cattle, with rusty chains still hanging in the stalls, festooned with cobwebs in which bits of chaff hung and whirled with every draught, as if frantic to escape from the ever-vigilant spiders. At the other end was a room up an outside stone stair. A large, long room with a sooty blackened fireplace and a very small window, also darkened with cobwebs and chaff. Once, the whole hill-farmer's family had lived in it for eating and sleeping and everything. Now it was the nearest thing Ralph had to an office.

Ralph climbed the outside stair, and looked round the room fondly. There was no furniture except an old weathered grey table, two three-legged stools, and a pile of logs for the fire, that could be sat on, if necessary. But ancient harness hung on the walls; blackened brass and leather so brittle it snapped in your hand like potato-crisps. Jack Norton had told him to chuck it out; but he'd kept it because he liked to see it hanging there. Otherwise there were two greasy beer-bottles, half-full of tractor-fuel for lighting the fire; and the old grey mattress in the corner, where Ralph slept during the lambing-season.

Jack Norton never came here, except once a year for the shearing and sheep-dipping. The rest of the time Ralph felt his own boss; nearly a farmer already. He had dreams of buying Pasture House, and living there one day . . .

But the job at the moment was checking how much sheep-dip he had. If Jack wasn't nagged in good time, he always forgot to buy more. Then he would drive off to fetch it on the morning of dipping-day, meet some feller in a pub, and they'd all be left standing round till after lunch . . .

Well, there were two five-gallon drums in the corner, left over

141

from last year. Ralph hefted their yellow bulk, to make sure they were full. They were both *nearly* full, standing in dark rings of their own chemical. He had *nearly* enough not to bother Jack at all . . .

Then he remembered there was another yellow drum lying outside, by the dipping-trough itself. Empty, or half-full?

Going back down the outside stair, he immediately looked across to see what the army were up to, on the other side of the Alston road, nearly a mile away. He couldn't see much at this distance; just a couple of bulldozers crawling up the slope, slow as woodlice. But the weight of Sephotic's tomb lay on his mind, heavy as lead. *How* could he warn Theloc?

He hadn't a clue. After a long while, he walked down to the dipping-trough. It was like all dipping-troughs, a stone slot set in the ground, about twenty feet long, two feet wide and four feet deep. They were always set so a little burn ran through them, in at one end and out the other. When you blocked the hole at the bottom end, the trough filled up with water by itself, which saved a lot of backache. Then you poured in the sheep-dip, mixing it well in till it turned the water a murky green.

There was a sheep-pen at each end of the trough, that would hold about twenty sheep. You pushed the sheep into the trough backwards, one by one. They were a long frantic time getting turned round and swimming to the far end, because sheep were stupid and panicky-bad swimmers. So they got well-soaked with dip. And, as they swam, people stood each side of the trough and used forked sticks to shove the sheep's heads under water, so their heads got dipped as well. It was cruel, a bit. Some cruel buggers enjoyed half drowning the sheep a lot. But it saved the sheep getting scab or red-mite, or that awful whicking with blow-fly maggots. So it was really kinder in the end.

When the sheep had scrambled out the far end, they were kept in the other pen for a few minutes, shaking themselves and dripping, so the spare chemical ran back down the ramp into the trough. Waste not, want not. Then that lot of sheep were released into the ten-acre field to graze and wait for the rest to be done.

He reached down and picked up the yellow drum. Half-full. He had enough after all, without bothering Jack. Providing it *was* sheep-dip. With Jack's sloppy ways, it was just as likely to be tractor-fuel . . .

He poured a bit out. No, it was sheep-dip all right. Nearly the same green as the paste in Prepoc's egg . . .

142

It was then the idea came to him. The only way to fetch Theloc was to fetch the Wawaka first. And the only way to fetch the Wawaka was to let loose some of that special radiation from Prepoc's belongings. That always fetched them; after a bit. And then, a bit later still, Theloc would turn up. The problem was, how to keep the Wawaka running round in harmless circles till Theloc *did* turn up?

And he suddenly had the answer. He felt terrified, and yet jubilant. The idea of saving the universe with a trickle of sheep-dip really tickled his fancy.

CHAPTER 20

Once a year, the loneliness of Pasture House was broken by a great event. Today was dipping-day, the high-point of Ralph's year.

The pens held nearly a thousand sheep. The look of them would not have pleased a townsman. Nothing like the Pure New Wool sheep on the telly. For they'd been sheared these last two days, and looked near-naked with long, scrawny necks like a giraffe's and great rounded pot-bellies. And not more than an eighth of an inch of glistening wool left on their skins.

But that wool shone white; for the smoke of Huddersfield and Leeds, that turns even the sheep on the high fells a darkish grey, had never reached the wool next to the sheep's skin.

Ralph could never get over the miracle of shearing; the bleating ewe held helpless on her back as the shears snipped and her six-inch fleece fell away, a frothing sea of white-gold within. Then the ewe was released, kicked out once on her golden bed, then fled naked from her frothing treasure, with no more than a bloody nick from the shears to remind her of her ordeal.

The year-old tups had been neutered, and branded with the farmer's initials their horns. No fun holding a hundred frantically struggling tups between your legs, while the red-hot branding-iron came down between your own bare straining wrists and bit into the horn, sending up a twist of dark-grey smoke and that smell that reminded Ralph of Hell as it was preached in chapel . . .

Then each farmer had come forward and marked his own sheep, with dabs of red dye from a blunt stick on their pearly skins. One dot for Norton; two for Austen; a bar for Mason and a vee for Umpleby. Because not all these sheep were Jack Norton's, though they all came from his fell. Sheep jumped the highest walls in their panics. Most were Norton's, but sixty were Mason's, forty-seven Umpleby's and thirty-one Austen's; with smaller numbers from farms further away.

Now, each farmer had come to help with the dipping, and take his sheep away with him afterwards. It was something of a picnic, for

144

the farmers' kids had come to help, and the farmers' wives sat in the tailgates of shooting-brakes, with well-filled food-baskets and a bottle of something special. And the farmers would stand around in collars and ties for once, wearing new caps and with their sticks poking out from under their arms at dangerous angles.

It was the farmhands who did all the sweating.

'All set, Ralph?' called Jack Norton, from a circle of laughing farmers. He'd shaved for once; it gave his face the look of a badly harvested field of stubble.

'All set,' shouted Ralph. 'Ten gallons of dip in, an' two to spare . . .' He surveyed the surface of the full dipping-trough. The water was opaque yellow-green, with clots of bubbles and little bits of twig and leaf floating in it.

'Well stirred in?' shouted Jack. He was enjoying making a fuss, playing at being the captain of the ship.

It was the moment Ralph had been waiting for. 'I'll give it a last stir,' he shouted. And stooped for his stick. Which was lying on the folded radiation-bag. Just inside the bag was the red egg . . . As Ralph picked up the stick, he picked up the egg also. Shielding it with his body from the crowd, he flipped it open and dropped it into the trough, then stirred the water vigorously with his stick.

The water changed to a subtler, colder shade of green. The egg would be washed empty now; the dipping-water would be radioactive with that particular kind of radioactivity that was like no radio-activity on earth; that meant Fefethil, and drew the Wawaka like flies round a drain. Ralph glanced up at the innocent blue sky. Are you up there, you bastards? Will you come for the bait?

'Come on, Ralph,' shouted Jack Norton. 'Stop bloody day-dreaming. We've got a few sheep to dip, here.' That got a laugh from the rest of the farmers. But not from the farmhands, who knew what an idle sod Jack was.

Ralph leapt into the pen where the sheep were waiting, bleating in a bored way, impervious to their fate. He grabbed the first sheep by its horns, and wheeled it backwards on its hind legs towards the mouth of the dipping-trough. He waited till the sheep's hind-legs fell scrabbling over the edge, then flung the front half of its body after them. As the sheep fell, its stupid face and mad, oblong eyes stared up at him for a second; then vanished beneath the water in an explosion of pale green foam.

And another; and another. He got into the rhythm of it; sheep

145

after sheep went sploshing in. The trough was full of bobbing, soaking woolly backs, being pushed under the surface again and again by vigorous thrusts of forked sticks. Then Ralph's pen was empty, and the far one full of sheep dripping like taps, and the green water was running back down the channels of the pen-floor and pouring back into the trough like a waterfall.

'Let 'em go,' shouting Jack Norton, whooping like some stupid cowboy at a rodeo. How many had he had this morning, from his hip-flask and other people's?

Someone opened the gate, and the first bunch of radioactive sheep was belting up the ten-acre field for all it was worth, desperate to get away from the vile water and the devils with forked sticks . . .

Twenty more bunches like that, thought Ralph, and the Wawaka won't know which to grab first. If they don't come too soon . . .

'Come on, Ralph. Bloody day-dreamin' about Ruby again?' That got a laugh from everybody.

They'll laugh on the other side of their faces when the Wawaka come, thought Ralph viciously. But already the gate of his own pen had been re-opened, and again he was knee-deep in sheep for the dipping. He put his back into it with a will. Safety in numbers!

The rate of dipping was always set by the man who threw the sheep in. All the others had to do was move the sheep from pen to pen. Ralph, as the resident shepherd, always threw in for the first hour. He was always brisk, not caring for hanging about yakking like some. But that morning he excelled himself, working faster than he had dreamed of before. And in between every pen-full, he wiped his forehead and watched the sky with a dry mouth. Sometimes the Wawaka came quicker than others times . . .

At the end of the first hour, they hadn't come; and the ten-acre was scattered with two hundred and forty radioactive sheep, who had doubtless covered the grass with radioactive drippings. Some grazing in little groups of four or five, some singly. *Quite* a problem for the Wawaka . . .

But not enough yet; not by half. Ralph refused to be relieved and went on like greased lightning.

'By, he's keen,' shouted Jack Norton. 'He'll have us finished by lunch-time at this rate! Mebbe he's hoping to have the afternoon off wi' that lass . . . He's got another think coming – there's a fence needs mending over Threlkeld's ... she can go and hold his fence-posts for him if she likes ...'

That got a rare laugh. It also reminded Ralph it was half-day closing, and Ruby would soon be around. She'd almost certainly walk up to watch the dipping. Ralph swore under his breath; he'd reckoned on having her safe in Penrith ... He threw in even faster.

Something else was worrying him too. He'd hoped, by throwing in the sheep carefully, to keep himself dry. But among so many sheep there were always the awkward buggers, that twisted and wriggled as they fell, making god-awful splashes. His whole front was now soaked with radioactive sheep-dip, from hair to boots. And he wasn't the only one. The blokes who were pushing the sheeps' heads under water were pretty well soaked too. Especially those working each side of Johnny Sligo ... If the Wawaka started grabbing everything radioactive ... Johnny Sligo in a mould-cupboard ... Ralph threw in faster still.

So fast that those moving the sheep from pen to pen couldn't keep up. Halts and stoppages, when Ralph could only stare fearfully at the empty blue sky.

'I think t'lad's in for t'Olympic record ...' Another laugh.

Still, after two hours, there were five hundred dripping sheep.

And still Ralph refused to be relieved. The idea of having to stand watching someone like Sligo wasting time, arsing about, was unbearable. He was in a muck-sweat now, hair flogging in his eyes. The ribbed concrete floor of the pen was slippery with dip and trampled sheep-droppings. Twice, but for his hobnailed boots, he would have fallen.

'Tea-break,' shouted Jack, sipping from a hip-flask that contained anything but tea.

They'd be stopped twenty minutes now. Everyone except Ralph flopped on to the grassy bank, swigging cold tea from beer-bottles and lighting up carefully hoarded fag-ends. Ralph could not sit still; he paced up and down, watching the sky, the field, the sheep. Feeling Jack's sneering eyes on him.

'Oh what it is to be young,' called Jack. 'All that energy!'

'What do you feed him on, Jack? Monkey-glands?'

'He'll be wantin' to tek whole farm off you next, Jack. Hardworking young feller like that!'

'You wanna watch out, Jack. Hard work might be infectious!'

The silly laughter echoed up and down the pens; if only the fools knew . . . Ralph stalked off, amidst laughter. Went higher up the burn, where it was deep, and flung himself in, desperately trying to wash the radioactivity off his boots, his trousers, his hair. And all the time a voice in his head repeating 'Coward! Why don't you warn *them* to wash as well?'

When he heard Jack's voice, calling people back to work, he got out of the burn reluctantly. As he did so, he saw somebody running away; somebody who had been spying on him . . . Sligo.

When he got back to the pen, he heard Sligo telling the rest: 'Chucked himself into't burn, like an overheated sheepdog.'

'Watch you don't give yourself colic, Ralph,' shouted somebody. But nobody laughed. They were all looking at him strangely, as if they thought he was mad. Ralph started throwing sheep in again, his rage and fear driving him faster than ever.

But after the third hour, his fear began to fade; to be replaced by another. Eight hundred sheep in the field, and still the Wawaka hadn't come. There hadn't been enough green paste left; the dip was too diluted to be really radioactive. And just to make it worse, the level in the trough had got too low. Jack let in more water, and added the last two gallons of sheep-dip, topping up.

You could top up the dip; but there was no way of topping up the radioactivity. Ralph was suddenly sick of the whole silly business. He just wanted to be away from the slippery concrete, and the over-powering smell of dip and sheep-shit; the heat, the endless noise of bleating and laughing. Bitterly, he threw the harder . . .

As the last fifty sheep approached, and the pens grew empty, all the spectators began to gather round in a crowd. Like the end of a half-marathon or something. Men began to pull out their watches, and reckon it was a record. As Ralph's pen was filled for the last time, the kids began to cheer him on.

But Ralph paused. Jack Norton had pulled his last dirty trick of the day. There were only twelve sheep in the last lot, and three of them were rams. Rams were twice the size of ewes, four times as strong, and they weren't terrified, but bloody aggressive. They'd go for you, given half a chance. Normally, when there was a single ram in a full pen, it was easy. You edged him towards the trough while he was packed in and helpless among the other woolly bodies . . .

There was no hope of that now; the pen wasn't full enough. All the sheep, instead of standing bleating, were whirling round in violent motion, panicky. Ralph braced himself and watched patiently, and took his first chance; a ram paused momentarily on the very edge of the trough. Ralph gave one dive, and down into the dip it went, though Ralph nearly followed it headfirst.

The crowd cheered; everyone knew what was going on. One up to Ralph! They were on his side really; Jack Norton wasn't very popular.

And then he was in trouble. The sheep were really wild now, all of them. Round and round and round they went. Ralph's legs felt as wobbly as india rubber bands; his guts ached with heaving; his hands felt paralysed with gripping so much horn and woolly skin. He wasn't going to make it; he was going to have to ask for help, and Jack would have the last laugh . . .

He was saved by the sheer unpredictability of sheep.

The second ram jumped in of its own accord, and began to swim vigorously towards the far end. The crowd whooped.

'Lad's a genius – he'm *psychin'* them in, now.'

'He'll be walkin' on't watter next!' Many forked sticks reached out, to drive the luckless ram under the dip.

One more. Now or never. Try full-frontal attack. He walked over to the ram and grabbed it by its horns and got it half-way to the trough in the first rush, before it regained its wits. Then it braced its legs and began to push him back. He braced his legs in turn, gained an extra two yards, and the pair of them hung balanced for a long moment on the verge of the trough, like hero and villain over a bottomless abyss at the end of a crime-movie.

Then his feet slipped and he fell full-length on his face in the green slime. But he had enough wit not to let go of its horns . . .

It began to drag him round the pen. The other sheep, frantic, ran across his back and legs. He saw the mouth of the trough passing and got to his knees and tried to push the ram in.

And fell on his face again. He could hear the crowd cheering and laughing like a mad thing.

'Ride'm, cowboy! Yeeh heeeeeeh!'

The ram paused. Big though it was, it couldn't go on dragging Ralph round for ever. And it paused very close to the trough. Ralph rose to his knees again, gave one last heave that made him think he had ruptured himself for certain, and the ram went in, in a splather of foam.

Then immediately jumped straight out again and ran into the crowd, shaking itself vigorously. Then everyone was after it, men and women, kids and dogs, in a joyous hunt round the pens.

Eventually, they cornered it. Paralysed by such a crowd of enemies, it went rigid, and was dragged back by many willing hands and thrown in, amidst great rejoicing.

Ralph just stood watching; then threw in the last nine ewes without trouble, they were so weary and cowed.

Then the sheepdogs were thrown in, to stop them getting ticks from the sheep. At least so it was said; Ralph just thought people were having so much fun, they didn't want to stop. Then Johnny Sligo threw little Tommy Potts in. Then everyone else got together and threw Johnny Sligo in . . .

The crowd at last drew breath, delirious with happiness and soaked to the skin. Ralph was loudly clapped as he climbed out of the pen, so stiff he could hardly walk.

'Half-past one,' said Jack Norton, very miffed. 'Lunch-time.' And drained his hip-flask to console himself.

Most settled on the grass with their food-baskets. Others had work to do. Mason's lad got his soaking dogs, and began to drive off his father's small herd. Austen began to get his into his big cattle-truck.

And then something got in the way of the sun.

Two huge mirror-ships, hovering a hundred feet above the field.

CHAPTER 21

Ralph glanced down, from the mirror-ships to the people on the ground.

His was the only movement; everybody else was frozen; by the huge things that could not possibly be there. Jack Norton with somebody else's flask in his hand; Mrs Norton with an arm stretched out, passing a sandwich to Billy. Togger Smurthwaite, legs apart and gap-toothed mouth gaping. All frozen, as a young leveret freezes, when the shadow of a hawk passes over it.

No movement in the mirror-ships either. Ralph knew that they *were* baffled, by the amount, the diffuseness, of the radiation. Like he'd guessed, they didn't know what to start picking up first.

It gave him a little confidence. He'd be able to move, once he'd worked out what to do.

Slowly, trapdoors opened in the undersides of the mirror-ships; like an air-liner putting down its wheels before landing; objects protruded . . .

On the ground, the frozen crowd crouched lower; as a young leveret does when the shadow of the hawk comes nearer.

Then there was a bang, a bar of light from mirror-ship to earth. A small flock of sheep, and the grass they'd been grazing on, simply vanished, leaving a round crater such as a small bomb might have left.

A whimper came from the frozen crowd, and that was all.

Bang, flash. Another small group of sheep vanished; nearer. And another; and another.

Now Ralph was running; now he knew what he had to do. He had only one more card to play, and he played it. He pulled the bung out of the dipping-trough, and the radioactive dip began to run down the burn, with the speed of a running man . . .

That caught their interest, above. A whole sequence of bangs and flashes as the mirror-ships ate up the burn. A louder bang, and the dipping-trough itself was gone, as the sewage-farm had gone so long

151

ago. Then the white beams were playing among the sheep again. Then Mason's herd vanished from the green-road, and Mason's lad with it . . . Then Austen's cattle-truck was suddenly no longer there.

Now the people were running and screaming, scattering in all directions. And the terrible white rays were among them, picking them off one by one. Mrs Norton, Jack, Billy . . .

Ralph just stood there, no longer caring for his own safety. He didn't deserve any safety. He had murdered them all; as he had murdered Postie.

For a moment, the banging and flashing stopped. Through the silence, Johnny Sligo came staggering, his mouth gaping, his out-stretched fingers groping, eyes staring fixedly, until he saw Ralph.

'Where are they?' he shouted. 'Where *are* they? Where have they gone?'

Then he flung himself on his face, fingers clawing at the earth as if to convince himself that *that* was still real.

Another bang and a flash.

And half of Johnny Sligo was gone. Where his outstretched legs had been was now the edge of a crater. But his eyes still pleaded with Ralph, more alive than ever. His fingers still groped. While his blood ran down the crater's smooth side, soaking into the earth like red rain.

And then another, longer silence, that went on and on and on. The survivors were standing like statues. Jack Austen, his wife and daughter Jean, with their arms around each other . . . and a sheepdog frozen in midstride . . .

Then Ralph looked up and saw the Fefethil ships. Four of them, and they held the mirror-ships in a web of beams.

And still the Austens stood like statues; and Ralph realized only he could move.

He began to run up between the craters in the ten-acre, to where the black ships hovered.

'Theloc! Theloc!'

But black ships and mirror-ships were drifting away from him, slowly as clouds, towards the fell where the army-camp lay.

Madly he ran after them, shouting and waving. 'Theloc, wait! I've found it. I've found it!' He did not remember where he ran. He must have climbed gates and walls, but he could never afterwards remember. Still the great ships moved away, as slow as clouds; but he had never realized how quick the slow drift of clouds was.

He stopped running when the stitch in his side became unbearable; when he could no longer breathe.

All those dead; and still Theloc wouldn't listen . . .

And then blackness.

He was lying on a hard bed with his eyes shut; there was something thin and plastic clamped over his skull, stretching from ear to ear.

He opened his eyes, in terror of Wawaka. But only the solemn faces of Theloc and Thmeses stared down at him.

'Am I going to die?' he asked.

'Much worse,' said Theloc through the headphones. 'You are going to live.'

Then he remembered the carnage at Pasture House.

'I don't want to go back there, ever,' he said. 'I want to come with you.'

'You cannot,' said Thmeses gently. 'We have damaged your mind too much already.'

'I don't want to live with . . . apes . . . any more.'

'That is the damage we have done to your mind. It would be much better if you forgot us. You are an ape, and must live out your life with apes. We can make you forget *everything* . . .'

'No. I want to remember. I want to remember *all* of you . . .'

'We will allow you to remember us. If you will go back to the other apes.'

'Apes are *mad*. Apes kill apes. Why don't you *stop* them? You know you could do it. Then we'd have peace all over the world . . .'

'Oh, yes, we could *do* it,' said Theloc. 'We have a chemical. If we released it into your atmosphere, in three days all apes would become as harmless as sheep.'

'Why don't you do it, then?'

'The Lord Merethon would not approve. There is not a world in all the universe where *sheep* have achieved anything. Sheep . . . remain . . . sheep. Apes may yet have something to give to the universe. That is Lord Merethon's hope.'

Yet Ralph felt that Theloc spoke out of duty and loyalty, not conviction.

'Will I see you again? When you come for Sephotic's tomb?'

'Sephotic's tomb is gone already. Sephotic will be buried in a . . . safer . . . place.'

153

'And Prepoc?'

'All of Prepoc is gone, too. Even the red egg in your dipping-trough. You will never be bothered by Wawaka again.'

A terrible feeling of grey boredom settled over Ralph; as if it was Monday morning and raining, all over the universe . . .

'That is your illness speaking,' said Thmeses. 'That is the memory that will hurt you all your life. Your life will be much happier, if we take away your memory . . .'

'No,' said Ralph.

'Very well,' said Theloc. 'Three gifts we will give you. The first concerns the ape Ruby. She was taken by the Wawaka . . . she was still radioactive.'

Ralph covered his face with his hands. Could there be any *more* pain in the universe?

'Fortunately, we were able to recover her in time. She was nearly dead. We put her in the healing machine we put you in. Without her permission, for she was unconscious. She is now entirely well, and her body purged of harmful chemicals and imbalances. She is in peak mating condition, as you are yourself. We suggest that for the sake of your offspring, you mate as soon as possible . . .'

There was a slight movement of Fefethil ears that might have been humour. 'And here,' said Theloc, 'is your second gift.'

It appeared to be an old, worn haversack, the sort farmworkers carried their lunch in. Full of old dry leaf-mould.

'*Thank you*,' said Ralph, with a staunch politeness that would have warmed Mam's heart.

'We know you dislike the hunting of the fox. If you drop the smallest particles of those leaves in front of the hounds' noses, they will run in circles for hours. Quite happily, of course.'

Ralph laughed out loud; when he had thought he might never laugh again.

'It is time for you to go,' said Theloc. The Fefethil came and rubbed their cheeks against Ralph's, in farewell . . .

'Hey, what about my third present?' shouted Ralph, like some greedy kid on Christmas morning. He wasn't really greedy; he was just putting off the time when he would never see them again.

'That you will discover in good time. Now we must go. There is a distress call from the Ulumi . . .'

Then there was blackness again.

*

He was crossing the crest of the hill above Pasture House. He braced himself to face the horror.

There was no horror. The ten-acre was full of calmly grazing sheep, and there wasn't a crater in sight. The dipping-trough was in position and still full of green dip. The burn ran past it normally . . .

The families were sprawled on the grassy bank. All the kids had joined Johnny Sligo in a kickabout with a coke-tin. Johnny was showing off, not letting the kids get near the tin. While the dogs lay in the shadow of the cars, their tongues lolling at such noonday folly.

Jack Norton leered up from a tartan rug. 'Been for a walk, Ralph? Bit o' exercise do you good, after a morning's loafin'?' His breath came up to Ralph; pure whisky-vapour you could've lit with a match.

'Anything happened?' asked Ralph, cautiously.

'Like what? If you haven't bin up to owt, we haven't. Our Billy had a dream o' flying saucers landing, an' waked up screamin'. Comes of all that lunch-time boozin'. When you get cleared up here, Ralph, there's that fence to mend, over Threlkeld's.' Having shown such generosity, he composed himself for further lunch-time slumbers.

Ralph shook his head, trying to clear it. How had the Fefethil done it? Like the cleaners after the school Christmas party. You left the school thinking it'd never be the same again, with all the spilt coke and food, and the way Timmy Starr had thrown up in the cloakroom. And when you got back next morning, for the final assembly, it was all cleaned up and smelling of polish, and the Christmas decorations put away till next year, and the Christmas tree, broken in half, sticking out of the dustbin . . .

He was just glad the Fefethil were on our side. Only they weren't on anybody's side really . . . Or everybody's . . . Had they put the soldiers on the fell to sleep as well?

Old man Austen drove off with his sheep in his cattle-truck, his dangerously dangling exhaust-pipe, held on only with binder-twine, further polluting the atmosphere of planet earth. The sheep inside baaed unhappily, on their way to slaughter. The families packed up, shouting roughly at their dogs, giving them the odd kick with a boot-toe, if they weren't quick enough getting about their business in the heat.

The arrogant apes, who never guessed how thin was the crust of safety they lived on; a crust they nibbled away at, every day . . .

Quiet at last. Ralph began to pick up the crisp-bags and beer-cans, and those endless bits of binder-twine that farmers leave everywhere.

Then he saw this girl coming up the green-road. He couldn't decide whether it was Ruby or not. She was tall and slim like Ruby. But she hadn't that stoop from the supermarket tills. And instead of bobbing humbly to the departing families as they drove past, she gave an airy wave, like the rich pony-girls Ralph sometimes saw. And she wasn't tottering on the wrong kind of shoes. She was striding out like a feller. She had too much energy to be Ruby; too much spring . . .

'Hi, Ralph!' Ruby's voice; and yet not Ruby's voice. Full of a tolerant humour. 'They left you to do the clearing up, as usual?'

He looked at her, and she looked back, and he felt strangely uneasy. She looked great; colour in her cheeks he hadn't seen before. But she was . . . bossy, somehow.

'What on earth you mooning at, Ralph?'

'You look smashing.'

'I feel smashing. Give me a kiss, you great idiot.' And without waiting for him, she landed him a smacking kiss. There she was, being bossy again.

She ought to wait for *him* to kiss *her* . . .

She frowned. 'What's up wi' you, then?'

'Nothing!'

'Funny kind of nothing! Ah, well, I expect you'll get over it. Let's get on. Too nice a day to waste moonin'.'

'When I've finished here, I've got a fence to mend, over Threlkeld's.' He enjoyed being awkward; expected her face to fall. That'd teach her to be so bossy . . .

'Who says?' she demanded, picking up bits of rubbish with great rapidity.

'Jack says . . .'

'Stuff Jack. He'll be drunk an' snoring b'now . . .'

'I've got work to do . . .'

'Nothing that can't wait. I want to go for a walk . . .'

'But . . .'

'But nothing. If you don't want to come, I'll go on my own. Then, when you're ready to treat me decent, you can come back and try again. *If* I'm still available . . .'

He looked at the brightness of her eyes, at the rich texture of her skin, and knew it was no idle threat.

156

'OK. I'll come,' he said grudgingly.

'You make a girl feel so *wanted*. OK, so what about some help clearing up this mess?'

He started picking rubbish up, knowing that things were going to be very different, and not sure he liked the difference.

Theloc's bloody health-machine . . .

A month later, on a Sunday, they climbed the fell again. The army had gone, three days before. There was a lot of rubbish marked W D.

Above, they climbed the slicing gullies that marked the battle. The sharp edges were crumbling; water was doing its work. Here and there, something green was sprouting out of the black peat. By next summer, the wounds would be healed.

A cairn of sorts was back in place; smaller and looking very raw and new. The army's work.

'Bet the lead-mine's gone,' said Ralph.

'Well, I want to see, anyway. I want to see everything there is to see . . .'

But Ralph was wrong; the entrance was still there, still blocked with Ralph's stones . . . Suddenly excited, he pulled them away. The way seemed shorter, by the light of the electric lantern Ruby had bought cheap in the autumn sales.

But when they reached the place where the smooth blaster-tunnel had been, it was gone. So was the yellow wall of Fefethil-metal.

But there was something. A small block of black marble, set into the middle of the rough sandstone, where the tunnel ended. With a golden sunburst on it, that glittered in the light of the lantern. And letters.

'RALPH EDWARDS + RUBY TODD
WHAT IS MAN THAT THOU ART MINDFUL OF HIM?'

'Like a tombstone,' said Ruby. 'A tombstone of the future.'

Ralph said nothing, just squeezed her hand.

'I'll bet that plus-sign means we *are* goin' to get married,' said Ruby, complacently.

But Ralph still stood silent; it was the word 'man' that kept catching his eye.

Not 'ape'. 'Man'.

He only wished they could have mentioned Postie.

Some other books you might enjoy

UNEASY MONEY
Robin F. Brancato

What would you do if you won a fortune? That's what happens when Mike Bronti buys a New Jersey lottery ticket to celebrate his eighteenth birthday. Suddenly, everything looks possible: gifts for his family, treats for his friends, a new car for himself – but things don't work out quite as Mike expects them to. A funny sensitive story about everyone's favourite fantasy.

THE TRICKSTERS
Margaret Mahy

The Hamiltons gather at their holiday house for their customary celebration of midsummer Christmas in New Zealand, but it is to be a Christmas they'll never forget. For the warm, chaotic family atmosphere is chilled by the unexpected arrival of three sinister brothers – the Tricksters.

THREE'S A CROWD
Jennifer Cole

How much fun can you have when your parents are away? No housework, no homework, a BIG party, and plenty of boys. Hey, who's throwing pizza around and where's Mollie disappeared to with that strange guy? (The first book in the *Sisters* trilogy.)

BREAKING GLASS
Brian Morse

When the Red Army drops its germ bomb on Leicester, the affected zone is sealed off permanently – with Darren and his sister Sally inside it. Immune to the disease which kills Sally, Darren must face alone the incomprehensible hatred of two of the few survivors trapped with him. And the haunting question is: why did Dad betray them?